MY STORYTIME TREASURY

MY STORYTIME TREASURY

EDITED BY

OLIVE BEAUPRÉ MILLER

Houghton Mifflin Company

Boston 1991

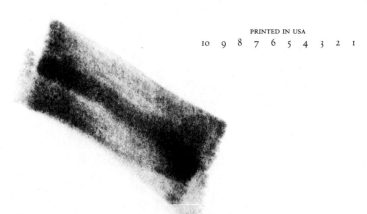

PREFACE

My Storytime Treasury is drawn from the pages of one of the oldest and best known anthologies of literature for children, My Book House. Collected and edited by Olive Beaupré Miller in 1919 in the USA, My Book House has entertained and introduced children to literature from all over the world ever since its origination over seventy years ago. It has never been out of print.

My Storytime Treasury is a special selection from My Book House for children two to five years of age. It begins with repetitive, short, rhythmic stories in prose with very simple plot, construction and wording. It acknowledges that it is not yet possible to hold the child's attention on any one subject for any length of time and that the charm of rhythm is a great factor in keeping interest. Accordingly, we have simple prose stories with a refrain repeated frequently like the one in "The Little Gray Pony":

"What *shall* I do? What *shall* I do?
If my little gray pony has lost a shoe?"

From this beginning we go on to give the child slightly longer and more complicated stories, constantly inviting a little more concentration and a little longer attention span.

In My Storytime Treasury you will find timeless classics like "The Little Engine That Could," "The Gingerbread Man," "The Night Before Christmas," and many more. From the classics of literature, there are Eugene Field's "Wynken Blynken and Nod" and his "Sugar Plum Tree," Dame Wiggins of Lee," by John Ruskin and Mary Sharpe, tales from "Aesop's Fables," "The Ugly Duckling" by Hans Christian Andersen, the ridiculous tale of Baron Munchausen. There are poems from John Keats, Vachel Lindsay, Walt Whitman, Christina Rossetti, Edward Lear and many others.

As a means of expression music appeals very strongly to children who feel its emotional appeal and its rhythm and harmony. My Storytime Treasury begins the process of introducing children to music as well as literature.

Thus for the old rhyme . . . .

> "Buzz, buzz, buzz . . .
> This is the song of the bee.
> His legs are all yellow,
> The jolly good fellow,
> A very hard worker is he!"

there is this footnote:

> "The Bee by François Schubert delightfully depicts in music the bee buzzing, darting from flower to flower and disappearing in a blossom."

In like manner for the poem, "Come Little Leaves," *The Whirlwind* by Krantz with its tone picture of leaves whirling in the wind is suggested; for "Ole Shut-Eyes," *The Dustman* by Brahms; for "Moon So Round and Yellow," Beethoven's *Moonlight Sonata* and Schumann's *Moonlight*; for "The Ugly

Duckling," *The Swan* by Camille Saint-Saens. And in addition to the notes on music, you will find in My Storytime Treasury the tale of the Nutcracker Suite for which Tchaikovsky wrote this Christmas ballet; the quaint little tale of how Chopin wrote his *Minute Waltz*, or *Little Dog Waltz*, from watching a little dog tear around after his tail; and the story of The Teddy Bears' Picnic, as John Bratton fancied it when he wrote the music in which one can hear the teddy bears march, growl, romp and play, then go home in perfect order.

Olive Beaupré Miller felt that very young children who were busy making sense of the world of reality around them were often confused by elves and fairies, not knowing where to place them in their thinking. My Storytime Treasury takes special care to keep a good balance by offsetting imaginative tales with tales of real life and by including humorous stories.

Among the stories we have here is "Oeyvind and Marit," by the Great Norwegian author, Bjornsterne Bjornson, "How The Brazilian Beetles Got Their Gorgeous Coats" from Brazil and "The Right Time To Laugh," from Australia.

The illustrations are as timeless as the text: simple and pretty, quaint and bright, but never garish.

Olive Beaupré Miller's object in creating this delightful collection of poems, fables and stories was to entertain and to introduce children in a systematic way to the written word and to entice them along the road to reading and enjoying for themselves.

Contents

The Little Red Hen
and the Grain of Wheat

AN ENGLISH FOLK TALE

THE Little Red Hen was in the farmyard
with her chicks looking for something to eat.
She found some grains of wheat and she said:

> "Cut, cut, cut, cudawcut!
> These grains of wheat I'll sow;
> The rain and warm spring sunshine
> Will surely make them grow.

Now who will help me sow the wheat?"

"Not I," said the Duck.

"Not I," said the Mouse.

"Not I," said the Pig.

"Then I'll sow it myself," said
Little Red Hen.   And she did.

When the grain had grown up tall and was ready to cut,
Little Red Hen said:

> "Cut, cut, cut, cudawcut!
> I'll cut, cut, cut this grain;
> It's nodding ripe and golden,
> From days of sun and rain.

Now who will help me cut the wheat?"
    "Not I," said the Duck.
    "Not I," said the Mouse.
    "Not I," said the Pig.
    "Then I'll cut it myself," said Little Red Hen
And she did.
    When the wheat was cut, Little Red Hen said:

> "Cut, cut, cut, cudawcut!
> It's time to thresh the wheat;
> Each little grain so precious
> From out the chaff I'll beat.

Now who will help me thresh the wheat?"
    "Not I," said the Duck.
    "Not I," said the Mouse.
    "Not I," said the Pig.
    "Then I'll thresh it myself," said Little Red Hen.
And she did.
    When the wheat was threshed, Little Red Hen said:

THE GRAIN OF WHEAT

"See where the windmill's great, long arms
  Go whirling round and round!
  I'll take this grain straight to the mill;
  To flour it shall be ground."

"Cluck! Cluck! Who'll help me carry the grain to the mill?"

"Not I," said the Duck.

"Not I," said the Mouse.

"Not I," said the Pig.

"Then I'll carry it myself," said Little Red Hen.
And she did.

When the wheat was ground, Little Red Hen said:

"I've sowed and reaped and threshed, cluck, cluck!
  I've carried to the mill,
  And now I'll bake a loaf of bread,
  With greatest care and skill.

Who'll help me bake the bread?"

"Not I," said the Duck.

"Not I," said the Mouse.

"Not I," said the Pig.

"Then I'll bake it myself," said Little Red Hen.
And she did.

When the bread was baked, Little Red Hen said:

> "Cluck, cluck! Cluck, cluck!
> The bread is done,
> It's light and sweet,
> Now who will come
> And help me *eat*?"

"I *will*," quacked the Duck.

"I *will*," squeaked the Mouse.

"I *will*," grunted the Pig.

"*No, you won't!*" said Little Red Hen. "Did you help
me sow and cut and thresh? Did you help me carry and
bake? No, you didn't! So you shall not help me *eat*! My
chicks will help me do that!"

And they did.

The Little Gray Pony*

MAUD LINDSAY

THERE was once a man who owned a little gray pony. Every morning, when the birds were singing, the man would jump on his pony and ride away, clippety, clippety, clap! The man rode to town and to country, to church and to market, up hill and down hill; and, one day, he heard something fall with a clang on a stone in the road. Looking back, he saw a horseshoe lying there. And when he saw it, he cried:

"What *shall* I do? What *shall* I do,
If my little gray pony has lost a shoe?"

Then down he jumped in a great hurry and looked at one of the pony's forefeet, but nothing was wrong. He lifted the other forefoot, but the shoe was still there. He examined

*From *Mother Stories*. Copyright, 1900. Used by kind permission of the publishers, Milton Bradley Company.

one of the hindfeet, and began to think that he was mistaken; but, when he looked at the last foot, he cried again:

> "What *shall* I do? What *shall* I do?
> My little gray pony has lost a shoe!"

Then he made haste to go to the blacksmith, and he called:

> "Blacksmith! Blacksmith! I've come to you;
> My little gray pony *has* lost a shoe!"

But the blacksmith answered and said:

> "How can I shoe your pony's feet,
> Without some coal the iron to heat?"

So the man left the blacksmith's, hurried here and there to buy the coal.

With phonograph records, the radio, or playing the piano, the mother can develop a love and appreciation of good music in her child. A good accompaniment to the story above is *The Wild Horseman* by Schumann which suggests the sound of horses' hoofs as they clatter along in a happy gallop.

THE LITTLE GRAY PONY

First of all he went to the store, and he said:

> "Storekeeper! Storekeeper! I've come to you;
> My little gray pony has lost a shoe!
> And I want some coal the iron to heat,
> That the blacksmith may shoe my pony's feet."

But the storekeeper answered and said:

> "Now I have apples and candy to sell,
> And more nice things than I can tell;
> But I've no coal the iron to heat,
> That the blacksmith may shoe your pony's feet.'

Then the man went away sighing, and saying:

> "What *shall* I do? What *shall* I do?
> My little gray pony has lost a shoe!"

By and by he met a farmer with a wagon, and he said:

Music, as a means of expression, appeals very strongly to children who, in their simplicity, feel the emotional appeal, the rhythm and beauty of harmony. The simplest music was the folk songs such as those in Volume I and from them developed the more complex symphonies.

"Farmer! Farmer! I've come to you;
My little gray pony has lost a shoe!
And I want some coal the iron to heat,
That the blacksmith may shoe my pony's feet."

But then the farmer answered and said:

"I've bushels of corn, and hay, and wheat,
Something for you and your pony to eat;
But I've no coal the iron to heat,
That the blacksmith may shoe your pony's feet."

So the farmer drove away and left the man sighing:

"What *shall* I do? What *shall* I do?
My little gray pony has lost a shoe!"

But, in the farmer's wagon, the man had seen corn, which made him think of the mill; so he ran to the mill, and called:

"Miller! Miller! I've come to you;
My little gray pony has lost a shoe,
And I want some coal the iron to heat,
That the blacksmith may shoe my pony's feet."

THE LITTLE GRAY PONY

The miller came to the door in surprise, and he said:

"I have wheels that go round and round,
And stones to turn till the grain is ground;
But I've no coal the iron to heat,
That the blacksmith may shoe your pony's feet."

Then the man turned away sorrowfully, and sat down on a rock near the roadside, sighing and saying:

"What *shall* I do? What *shall* I do?
My little gray pony has lost a shoe!"

After a while a very old woman came down the road, driving a flock of geese to market; and, when she came near the man, she stopped to ask him his trouble. He told her all about it; and, when she had heard it all, she laughed till her geese joined in with a cackle and she said:

"If you would know where the coal is found,
You must go to the miner, who works in the ground."

Then the man sprang to his feet, and, thanking the old woman, he ran to the miner. Now the miner had been working many a long day down in the mine, under the ground where it was so dark that he had to wear a lamp on the front of his cap to light him at his work. He had plenty of black coal ready and gave great lumps of it to the man, who took them in haste to the blacksmith.

The blacksmith lighted his great, red fire, and hammered out four, fine new shoes, with a cling and a clang. And fastened them on with a rap and a tap! Then away rode the man on his little gray pony—clippety, clippety, clap!

A Winky-Tooden Song

O HERE'S a little rhyme
    for the Spring or Summer-time—
An a-ho-winky-tooden-an-a-ho!
Just a little bit o' tune
    You can twitter, May or June,
An a-ho-winky-tooden-an-a-ho!

It's a lovely little thing
That 'most any one could sing
With a ringle-dingle-ding,
    Soft and low, don't you know,
An a-ho-winky-tooden-an-a-ho!

          —James Whitcomb Riley

From *Book of Joyous Children*, by James Whitcomb Riley, copyright 1902, 1930.
Used by special permission of the publishers, The Bobbs-Merrill Company.

Wynken, Blynken, and Nod*

EUGENE FIELD **

Wynken, Blynken, and Nod one night
  Sailed off in a wooden shoe—
Sailed on a river of crystal light,
Into a sea of dew.
"Where are you going, and what do you wish?"
The old moon asked the three.
"We have come to fish for the herring-fish
That live in this beautiful sea;
Nets of silver and gold have we!"
Said Wynken, Blynken, and Nod.

*From *Poems of Eugene Field*; copyright, 1910, by Julia Sutherland Field. Published by Charles Scribner's Sons. **In a study full of the toys of his seven children, Eugene Field, American, (1850-1895), wrote his beautiful poems of childhood.

The old moon laughed and sang a song,*
As they rocked in the wooden shoe,
And the wind that sped them all night long
Ruffled the waves of dew.
The little stars were the herring-fish
That lived in that beautiful sea—
"Now cast your nets wherever you wish—
But never afeared are we!"
So cried the stars to the fishermen three;
Wynken, Blynken, and Nod.

All night long their nets they threw
To the stars in the twinkling foam—
Then down from the skies came the wooden shoe,
Bringing the fishermen home;
'Twas all so pretty a sail, it seemed
As if it could not be,
And some folks thought 'twas a dream they dreamed
Of sailing that beautiful sea—
But I shall name you the fishermen three;
Wynken, Blynken, and Nod.

Wynken and Blynken are two little eyes,
And Nod is a little head,
And the wooden shoe that sailed the skies
Is a wee one's trundle-bed.
So shut your eyes while mother sings
Of wonderful sights that be,
And you shall see the beautiful things
As you rock on the misty sea,
Where the old shoe rocked the fishermen three;
Wynken, Blynken, and Nod.

*This lullaby has been set to music. The lulling of children, the soft crooning of mothers to their babies created some of the earliest folk songs, and lullabies are among the most beautiful compositions of the great musicians.

Ole Shut-Eyes, the Sandman[*]

ADAPTED FROM HANS CHRISTIAN ANDERSEN

ONE night a little boy named Hjalmar went to bed. And when he was fast asleep, a jolly old fellow, dressed in shiny clothes of many colors, came softly into his room. The jolly old fellow was Ole Shut-Eyes, the Sandman, the man who makes children feel sleepy. He came and sat on Hjalmar's bed to tell him a story while he was asleep. Now no one in all the world can tell children such good stories as Ole, the Sandman. He held over Hjalmar's head a beautiful umbrella with many pictures on it, for it's only when children are under the Sandman's umbrella that they can hear what he says in their dreams.

*Music to be played with *Ole Shut-Eyes, the Sandman*, might be *The Dustman* by Brahms, other of the beautiful lullabies for which Brahms was so famous, or Schubert's *Cradle Song*

"Hjalmar," the Sandman said, "I tell you what! I'll show you a little mouse!" Then he opened his fingers and look! Standing up on his hand was a tiny little mouse all dressed in the clothes of a lady.

"She has come to ask you to go to a party," the Sandman said. "It's a wedding party, Hjalmar. Two little mice are going to be married. Their wedding is to be held beneath the floor of your mother's pantry."

"Oh! I want to go! I want to go!" Hjalmar cried. "But I can't get through the floor! I'm far too big to squeeze through a mousehole!"

"Leave that to me," said the Sandman. "I'll soon make you small enough!" He touched Hjalmar with his wand, and the boy grew smaller and smaller till he was not as tall as one's finger. And then the Sandman said, "Now you must take the uniform from your little tin soldier. I think it will just about fit you, and be the very thing for a wedding."

So Hjalmar dressed up in his tin soldier's clothes. And didn't he feel grand in a uniform like that! Then he saw that the little mouse was standing by his mother's thimble.

"Please get into this thimble," she said, "and I'll draw you to the wedding."

So Hjalmar thanked her politely and climbed in the thimble. Then the little mouse wrapped her tail around the thimble so she could drag it along behind her and they started off on their way.

First they went down through the mousehole, right through the hole in the floor. Then they went along under the floor till they came to a long low passage, which was only just big enough for a thimble to be drawn through, but it was all very brightly lighted and made Hjalmar feel very gay.

"Just ahead," said the little mouse, "is the hall where the wedding is to be."

Well, at last they came to the hall and there, all together on one side, stood the little lady mice whispering and giggling merrily, and opposite stood all the gentlemen mice stroking their whiskers with their paws. The lovely little mouse maiden who was to be the bride and the handsome young man mouse who was to be the husband, stood in the center of the room in the round, hollow rind of a cheese kissing one another. More and more little mice kept pouring into the room, all dressed in their very best clothes and talking together merrily. By and by the mother and father of the little mouse bride and the mother and father of the little mouse groom stepped up to the circle of cheese rind and stood beside the young mice. Then a very old Mouse

Minister stood up before the pair and spoke the wedding words. Hjalmar stood by all the time looking on in his uniform.

After the wedding was over, there was a wedding supper. They didn't have a wedding cake, but a beautiful large green pea was brought in on a platter and on that pea the groom's brother had beautifully carved with his teeth the names of the bride and groom, that is, the first letter of each. It was a most happy wedding. Every single mouse said he had had a fine time and they all took their leave most politely.

When at last the party was over, Hjalmar drove home in the thimble and went to bed again. Next morning, he rubbed his eyes to think of the night before and of all the fine mouse company in which he had found himself. Of course, in the morning light, he didn't quite like to think that such a big boy as he had shrunk up so very small he could sit in his mother's thimble and wear the uniform of a little tiny tin soldier. "I am," he said to himself, "a very big boy indeed."

Little Gustava

CELIA THAXTER

LITTLE Gustava sits in the sun,
  Safe in the porch, and the little drops run
From the icicles under the eaves so fast;
For the bright spring sun shines warm at last.
    And glad is little Gustava.

She wears a quaint little scarlet cap,
And a little green bowl she holds in her lap,
Filled with bread and milk to the brim,
And a wreath of marigolds round the rim;
    "Ha! ha!" laughs little Gustava.

Up comes her little gray, coaxing cat,
With her little pink nose, and she mews, "What's that?"
Gustava feeds her—she begs for more,
And a little brown hen walks in at the door.
    "Good day!" cries little Gustava.

From *Stories and Poems for Children*. Used by permission of, and by special arrangement with Houghton, Mifflin Company.

LITTLE GUSTAVA

She scatters crumbs for the little brown hen.
There comes a rush and a flutter, and then
Down fly her little white doves so sweet,
With their snowy wings and their crimson feet.
 "Welcome!" cries little Gustava.

So dainty and eager they pick up the crumbs.
But who is this through the doorway comes?
Little Scotch terrier, little dog Rags,
Looks in her face and his funny tail wags.
 "Ha! ha!" laughs little Gustava.

"You want some breakfast, too?" And down
 She sets her bowl on the brick floor, brown;
 And little dog Rags drinks up her milk,
 While she strokes his shaggy locks, like silk.
 "Dear Rags!" says little Gustava.

MY STORYTIME TREASURY

Waiting without stood sparrow and crow,
Cooling their feet in the melting snow.
"Won't you come in, good folk?" she cried.
But they were too bashful, and stayed outside,
    Though "Pray come in!" cried Gustava.

So the last she threw them, and knelt on the mat
With doves, and biddy, and dog, and cat.
And her mother came to the open house door;
"Dear little daughter, I bring you some more,
    My merry little Gustava!"

Kitty and terrier, biddy and doves,
All things harmless Gustava loves.
The shy, kind creatures 'tis joy to feed,
And oh, her breakfast is sweet indeed
    To happy little Gustava!

The Two Crabs

ADAPTED FROM AESOP*

ONCE upon a time there was a Great Big Crab and once upon a time there was a little bit of a Crab. And the Big Crab used to come out of the sea and walk along on the sand of the beach. And the Little Crab used to come out of the sea and walk along on the sand of the beach also. So the Big Crab and the Little Crab would walk along together and the great green lobsters and the starfish and all the other creatures of the sea would stand in a row to watch them.

Now the Big Crab thought himself a very big crab indeed. He rolled his eyes about to see who was looking at him whenever he went out to walk. But, one day, when he was

*The slave boy, Aesop, told animal fables in Greece about 600 B.C. Although his tales were not written down till long after his death, they have lived through the ages and been translated into many languages.

33

swaggering along the beach, thinking how fine he looked, he chanced to look down at the Little Crab. Then he saw that the Little Crab was walking queerly. Waddle, waddle, twist and hitch the Little Crab was going.

"Dear me! Dear me!" the Big Crab said to himself. "Nobody will think much of me if they see me with such a poor Little Crab who doesn't know how to walk but goes along waddle, waddle, twist and hitch and waddle!"

So the Big Crab said to the Little Crab: "Child, you walk very queerly, twisting all the time and waddling from side to side. I hate to be seen in company with such a clumsy creature. Pray stop this waddle-waddle and walk in a straight line forward, one foot before the other."

Well, the Little Crab felt very sorry that his friend didn't like the way he walked. He wanted to learn to walk better. So he said, "I'll just look at the Big Crab and learn how to walk from him." Then he turned his eyes to look, and lo and behold, the Big Crab, the big, swaggering, uppity Big Crab, was going waddle, waddle, twist and hitch himself!

"Well, well, well!" said the Little Crab. "You waddle as much as I do! If you want me to walk straight, you must show me how, my friend, by first walking straight yourself! The only way to teach others how to do what is right, is just to do right yourself!"

Belling the Cat

ADAPTED FROM AESOP

LONG ago all the Mice came pattering from fields and pantries to hold a council meeting. They sat around under a washtub with a candle for a light and very solemnly asked: "What shall we do to keep ourselves safe from Pussy? She hides in secret places and suddenly springs out on us when we do not know she is near. What are we to do?"

Well, the Mice all wiggled their whiskers and blinked their eyes very gravely. Some said, "Let us do this!" And some said, "Let us do that!" But at last a young Mouse named Big Whiskers proudly rose to his feet.

"Friends," Big Whiskers said, feeling very sure that he knew more than all the rest, "I know just what we should do. Let us tie a bell by a ribbon around the neck of the Cat. Then she will not be able to move without jingling that little bell. Whenever we hear the bell tinkle, we will always know she is near and so we'll have plenty of time to scamper out of her reach." With this, Big Whiskers sat down twirling his showy mustache.

"Three cheers for Big Whiskers! We vote to follow his plan! Hurrah!" cried the other Mice and they all began to talk at once about whether to get a brass bell or whether to

get a silver bell, and whether to use a blue or a pink ribbon to tie the bell on the Cat. But at last, a very old Mouse, who had not spoken before, got up from his seat.

"Wait!" he cried in a voice that startled the rest like thunder. "Big Whiskers' plan is fine, but I've only this question to ask. Pray with all your talking, will one of you answer me this—who is going to be the one to put the bell on the Cat?"

For a moment the Mice looked foolish and nobody spoke a word. Who indeed would dare to go straight up to Pussy and tie the bell on her neck? Big Whiskers slunk away and hid himself in a corner. Not a single Mouse dared! Then the old Mouse looked around, peering up over his spectacles and very sadly he said: "It is all very well to *talk* about doing great things, but all that really counts is to *do* them."

36

c.m.c.

Reen-Reen-Reeny-Croak-Frog

A favorite tale of children in Colombia, South America

Young Reen-reen-reeny-croak-frog, he thought he was so fine;
He dressed up in his Sunday clothes and gave his shoes a shine.
In bright red suit and gay blue tie, he was most smartly dressed;
His hat, it had a ribbon and his vest, it was his best.
Just then his mother said, "My child, please don't go out today!"
But Reeny only tossed his head and straightway ran away.

As he was running down the road, he met Sir Mousie Mouse.
Said Mousie, "Friend, let's pay a call at yonder little house!
I'm off to visit Lady Mouse, so come along, pray do!
She always has a lot to eat, she'll have enough for you!"

They soon drew near the little house; Sir Mousie ran before,
And knock, knock!   With the knocker, he knocked upon the door.
"Who's there?" someone within the house now very sweetly cried.
"'Tis I, dear Lady Mouse!   'Tis I!" Sir Mousie Mouse replied.

So Lady Mouse, she oped the door in her most gracious way,
And Mousie said, "We've come to call. May we come in, I pray?"
With charming smile sweet Lady Mouse then bobbed her little head.
"Yes, yes! Come in! You're welcome! Please do come in!" she said.

Sir Mousie bowed and shook her hand and Reeny did so, too;
They greeted her politely just as gentlefolk must do.
She led them in the house and said, "Be seated in those chairs.
You both look well and Reeny here, how fine the suit he wears!"

And off she went for bread and cheese and for some nice cold meat.
And Reeny ate and ate and ate, as much as he could eat.
She brought in sugar cookies, too. He gobbled those as well,
With jam and every kind of sweet—more things than I can tell!

Then Lady Mouse said, "Reeny, would you sing a little tune?
Please sing a pretty song for me about the moon in June!"
But Reeny was too full to sing. He only croaked, "I vow
I'd like to sing, dear lady! But I really can't just now!"

"I'm very, very sorry!" Lovely Lady Mouse looked sad.
"I like to have my visitors make merry and be glad!
But since you cannot sing to me, I tell you what I'll do,
I'll sing a very pretty, very special song for you!"

So Lady Mouse, she sang a song and Mousie danced a jig,
But Reeny fell asleep because he'd eaten like a pig.
Then by-and-by he wakened, for he heard a loud, "Miaow!"
A cat and her two kittens! They had started up a row!

The cat was chasing Mousie so he ran and squeaked with fear.
"Miaow!" she cried. "Miaow! Miaow! I'll catch you by your ear!"
And while poor little Lady Mouse began to weep and wail,
The kittens, they chased after her to get her by her tail!

Then Reeny, seeing both his friends run here and there and weep,
Just took his hat and gave one big, tremendous, long, long leap!
He oped the door with hand and nose. He left them in a fright,
He only wished them, as he went, a very swift Good-night!

He jumped so high; he jumped so fast; he jumped so fast and high,
He lost his hat, he tore his shirt, he lost his Sunday tie!
He jumped straight into Mrs. Duck, a-waiting there, alack!
She cried, "I'll eat you up, I will! Quack, Quack! Quack, Quack!
    Quack, Quack!"

But Reeny bolted off for home.
    He raised an awful din—
"Oh, Mother! Save me! Mother dear!
    Oh, Mother, let me in!"
His mother saw him coming, pop!
    while Mrs. Duck gave chase;
She let him in and slammed the door in
    Mrs. Duckie's face!

Russian Rhymes

"DON'T run away my kitty,
In the carriage you must sit;
So stay there with my dollies
And ride around a bit!"

The little girl begged nicely
But Kitty ran away;
He said, "I'm very hungry,
I'll chase the mice today!"

"I'm going in to dinner!"
He jumped and off he ran—
"And after I have eaten,
Then catch me if you can!"

SNAIL, snail
Shakety shake
Put out your horns
And I'll give you some cake!

HARK, the Christmas bells are ringing
    And the children all are singing;
Dancing round the Christmas tree,
All as happy as can be!
See the candles shining bright,
Shining bright as stars of light,
And the goodies there to eat,
Little cakes and apples sweet!
All the pretty presents see
Lying there around the tree!

LITTLE bells, pretty flowers of the steppes,
    Turning your faces my way.
Why do you droop your heads
On such a bright May day?

As you shake your heads in the grasses,
What do you whisper and say?

—Колокольчики

41

The Magpie's Nest
AN ENGLISH FOLK TALE

ONCE on a time when pigs spake rhyme, the Thrush, the Owl, and the Blackbird, the Sparrow and the Turtle Dove, all came to call on Madge Magpie. They sat on the branches above her and all began to sing at once:

"Madge Magpie! Oh, Madge Magpie,
Pray will you teach us how
To build such nests as you do
Upon the swaying bough?

"There's no one in the tree-tops
Who knows so well as you
How birds should build their houses!
Caw, caw! Tu-whit, tu-whoo!"

So Madge Magpie flicked her tail
and blinked her eyes and said:

"Come sit in a circle about me,
If you'll listen I'll tell you how
To build just such nests as I do
Way up on the swaying bough."

42

First she took some mud and made it into a cake.
"Oh, that's how it's done, is it?"
cried the Thrush—

"Quit, quit, quit!
That's all there is to it!
I know it all! I know it all!
Quit, quit, quit!"

And off she flew in a hurry. So that's all the Thrush ever
learned about how to build a nest. Then Madge Magpie took
some twigs and twined them around in the mud.

"Oh, that's how it's done, is it?" cried the Blackbird.

"Mud and twigs! I saw! I saw!
I know it all! Caw, caw! Caw, caw!"

And off she flew in a hurry. So that's all the Blackbird ever
learned about how to build a nest. Then Madge Magpie put
another layer of mud over the twigs.

"Oh, I knew all that before I came," said the old Owl.

"Tu-whit, tu-whoo! I knew! I knew!
I'll build my nest as I always do!"

And away he flew in a hurry.
So that's all the Owl ever learned
about how to build a nest. Then Madge Magpie lined the
nest with feathers and soft stuff to make it snug and cozy.

"Oh, bother!" cried the Sparrow, "I've heard enough!"

"Chip, chip!
Chip! chip!
I know enough!
And now I'll skip!"

And away he flew in a hurry. So that's all the Sparrow ever learned about how to build a nest. Then Madge Magpie looked around and she saw that the only bird left was the Turtle Dove. But the Turtle Dove hadn't paid attention any of the time. She had just kept talking and talking herself. Madge had a twig in her mouth to weave around the outside of the nest to make it all firm and strong, when she heard that silly Turtle Dove crying: "Coo! Coo! Take two, Taffy, take two! Take two-o-o-o!" And Madge Magpie said:

"No, you don't take two. Take one! One's enough!"

But the Turtle Dove only said; "Coo! Coo! Take two!"

"One's enough, I tell you," cried Madge, "only one!"

But the Turtle Dove would not listen. She liked only to

talk herself! "Coo! Coo! Take two-o-o-o!"

And then Madge Magpie cried: "Alas! how can I teach silly birds to build nests if they will not *listen* to what I say?" And away she flew. Nor would she ever again tell any of them what to do.

The Goldfinch[*]

DOWN from the sky on a sudden he drops
    Into the mullein and juniper tops.
Lightly he sways on the pendulous stem,
Vividly restless, a fluttering gem,
Then with a flash of bewildering wings,
Dazzles away up and down, and he sings
Clear as a bell at each dip as he flies,
Bounding along on the wave of the skies.[*]

—Odell Shepard

Two Birds and Their Nest

TWO guests from Alabama—two together,
    And their nest, and four light-green eggs,
        spotted with brown,
And every day the he-bird, to and fro, near at hand,
    And every day the she-bird, crouch'd on her nest
        silent, with bright eyes,
And every day I, a curious boy,
        never too close, never disturbing them,
        Cautiously peering.

—Walt Whitman

*From A Lonely Flute. Used by permission of the publishers, Houghton, Mifflin Company.

Uncle Mitya's Horse

LEO N. TOLSTOY

UNCLE MITYA had a fine horse. He kept it in a pen that had a fence around it. But some thieves found out where he kept his horse and planned to steal it from him. Now it happened that night that a farmer came to visit Uncle Mitya and brought his pet bear with him. So Uncle Mitya let the horse out into the yard and put the bear in the pen where the horse had been.

In the dark the thieves came creeping. They stole up into the pen. But they found no horse there! What they found was that great big bear. The bear seized one of the thieves and how the fellow screamed! He screamed so loud Uncle Mitya heard him. Then Uncle Mitya and the farmer ran from the house and caught the thieves.

Johnny and the Three Goats

A NORSE TALE

NOW you shall hear! Once there was a boy named Johnny, and he had three goats. All day long those goats leaped and skipped and climbed way up on the top of a hill, but every night Johnny went to fetch them and drove them home. One evening the frisky things leaped out of the road, over a fence and into a turnip field, and, try as he would, Johnny could not get them to come out again. There they were and there they stayed. Then the boy sat down on the hillside and cried. As he sat there a hare came along.

"Why do you cry?" asked the hare.

"I cry because I can't get the goats out of the turnip field," answered Johnny.

"*I'll* get the goats out of the turnip field," said the hare. So he tried and he tried, but the goats would not come. Then the hare sat down beside Johnny and began to cry, too.

Along came a fox.

"Why do you cry?" asked the fox.

"I cry because the boy cries," said the hare, "and the boy

cries because he cannot get the goats out of the turnip field."

"*I'll* get the goats out of the turnip field," said the fox.

So the fox tried and he tried and he tried, but the goats would not come. Then the fox sat down beside Johnny and the hare and began to cry, too. Pretty soon along came a wolf.

"Why do you cry?" asked the wolf.

"I cry because the hare cries," said the fox, "and the hare cries because the boy cries, and the boy cries because he can't get the goats out of the turnip field."

"*I'll* get the goats out of the turnip field," said the wolf. So he tried and he tried and he tried and he tried, but the goats would not leave the field. So the wolf sat down beside Johnny and the hare and the fox and began to cry, too.

After a little a bee flew over the hill and saw them all sitting there crying for dear life, "Boo-hoo! Boo-hoo! Boo-hoo!"

"Why do you cry?" said the bee to the wolf.

THE THREE GOATS

"I cry because the fox cries," said the wolf, "and the fox cries because the hare cries, and the hare cries because the boy cries, and the boy cries because he can't get the goats out of the turnip field."

"Much good it does to sit there and cry about it," said the bee. "I'll get the goats out of the turnip field."

Then the great big wolf, and the great big fox, and the great big hare, and the great big boy all stopped boo-hooing a moment to poke fun at the tiny bee.

"You get the goats out of the turnip field when we could not! That's a joke! Ho, ho!"

But the tiny bee flew away into the turnip field and lit in the ear of one of the goats and all he did was say, "Buzz-z-z. Buzz-z-z. Buzz-z-z." And out ran the goats, every one!

49

The Donkey and the Lap Dog
ADAPTED FROM AESOP

ONCE a farmer went to his barn to see his favorite donkey, a great big shaggy gray animal, who was eating hay in a stall. Now the Donkey loved his master and as soon as he saw the man, he brayed: "Ee-aw! Ee-aw!"

"Good morning, yourself," said the man.

But, just at that moment a dog, a little teeny, tiny Lap Dog, came running out to the barn and began to frisk and leap and lick his master's hand.

"Hello, my pretty," said the Farmer. And he sat down on a bench, took the Dog up on his lap and began to pet and stroke him. Well, this was too much for the Donkey; he wanted the very petting the little Lap Dog was getting. So the Donkey said to himself, "Ee-aw! Ee-aw! Ee-aw! I do all the hard work while that little dog gets petted and hasn't a

50

thing to do. If I want the master to love me, I'll have to act like a lap dog." And all of a sudden that Donkey, that great, big, lumbering Donkey broke loose from his halter and began to caper about and frisk and dance and prance just like a little lap dog! He knocked over a pail of water! He banged into the master's bench. He upset a milking stool as he mimicked the little dog.

"What on earth are you doing?" the master howled in surprise while the little Dog ran in a fright.

Then the great, big, clumsy Donkey came leaping and jumping along and suddenly sat himself down right on the farmer's lap, just as the Lap Dog had done.

"Ee-aw, I want to be petted. Ee-aw! Ee-aw!" he said.

The Farmer began to laugh.

"You great, big clown!" he cried. "Go back to your stall and eat hay! If you want me to love you, you must be yourself and not act like anyone else."

And he led the Donkey back to his stall and stroked and petted him. "You're no good when you play the lap dog but you're a wonderful donkey," he said.

The Rooster and the Sultan

A HUNGARIAN FAIRY TALE

ONCE on a time there lived a very poor old woman who had nothing at all in the world except one Little Small Rooster. This Rooster was scratching the ground one day, looking for something to eat, when suddenly what should he find but a shiny penny! Now it chanced just then that a big fat man came along. He was called Sultan of the Land of Turkey and he came strutting up the street wearing big baggy pantaloons, red shoes with upturned toes and a bright red turban on his head. Well, the Sultan noticed the penny glittering there in the dust and he said to the Little Small Rooster, "Rooster, give me that penny!"

THE ROOSTER AND THE SULTAN

But the Little Small Rooster said, "No! I will give my mistress this penny, for she is poor and she needs it."

Then the Sultan snatched the penny away from the Little Small Rooster. He stuck up his nose in the air and he marched off home with the penny.

The Rooster was ready to cry, but he gave himself a good shake. He ruffled up his feathers as if getting ready to fight. He lifted his head up high, and he hurried after the Sultan. He ran into the Sultan's garden, and hopped up on the fence.

"Cock-a-doodle-doo!" he cried, "give me back my penny!"

What a noise! The Sultan clapped his hands to his ears. He ran as fast as he could to the most distant room in his great big, enormous palace. But the Little Small Rooster followed him and perched on his window sill.

"Cock-a-doodle-doo!" he cried. "Give me back my penny."

The Sultan got angrier and angrier. He called a slave and said, "Get that Rooster, slave, and throw him in the well!"

So the slave went and caught the Rooster and, bang! he plopped him in the well. But the Rooster kept his wits about him and began to say a charm:

"Suck the water up, my throat!
Suck the water, all the water. Suck the water up!"

So the Little Small Rooster's throat sucked up all the water and he was safe on dry ground. Then he flew to the Sultan's window. And once again he cried, "Cock-a-doodle-doo! Give me back my penny!"

Well, the Sultan was in a rage. He called a slave and said, "Go slave, get that Rooster and throw him in the fire!"

So the slave caught the Little Small Rooster and threw him in a roaring fire. But the Little Small Rooster cried:

"Pour out the water, my throat!
All the water, pour it! Put this big fire out!"

Instantly his throat poured all the water from the well into the leaping flames. The fire died down with a hiss. And the Rooster was safe again. Then he flew to the Sultan's window and cried as he had before, "Cock-a-doodle-doo! Give me back my penny!"

THE ROOSTER AND THE SULTAN

Well, the Sultan was now so angry he couldn't think what to do next. But he called a slave and said, "Go slave, get that Rooster and throw him in a bee-hive. The bees will sting him well! They'll end his terrible crowing!"

So the slave caught the Rooster again and threw him in a bee-hive. But the Rooster started singing:

"Suck the bees, my throat!
Suck the bees all up! Suck the bees all up!"

Then his throat sucked up the bees and the Little Rooster again rushed to the Sultan's window.

"Cock-a-doodle-doo!" he cried.
"Give me back my penny!"

The Sultan was beside himself! He just went raving mad. "Bring that Rooster to me!" he thundered.

So the slave went and caught the Rooster and brought him before the Sultan. And the Sultan, at sight of the Rooster, lost all the wits he had. He seized the Little Small Rooster and stuffed him into the pocket of his big, baggy pantaloons. "Now I have you, I'll keep you," he shrieked, "so you don't get out again!"

But the Little Small Rooster sang:

"Pour out the bees, my throat!
Pour the bees all out! Pour the bees all out!"

55

And his throat poured the bees all out in the Sultan's pantaloons. The bees began to sting the Sultan. They stung him and stung him and stung him. The Sultan screeched and he screeched! He slapped at his pantaloons! He danced on one foot! But he could not stop that stinging. So at last he yelled to a slave, "Give this Rooster back his penny and let him go from the palace! I must have peace again!"

So the slaves cut a great big slit in the Sultan's pantaloons. Out flew the Little Small Rooster and the swarm of angry bees. Then the Sultan heaved a sigh of relief. The slaves gave the Rooster his penny and let him go from the palace. And the Little Small Rooster flew home and gave the poor Woman the penny. The Old Woman bought all she needed to make herself cozy and comfortable and she and the Little Small Rooster lived happily ever after.

The Teddy Bears' Picnic*

from the Musical Composition by

JOHN W. BRATTON

ONCE the Teddy Bears had a picnic. They all started out together, marching very politely, right foot, left foot, right foot—a very orderly crowd. They were just too good for words when they started out on that picnic. No clock ever went tick-tock, tick-tock more regularly than those Teddy Bears went tramp, tramp as they marched slowly up the road.

When they got to the woods, they spread all their goodies out on a nice tablecloth on the grass and they sat around and they ate. They ate bread and butter and honey and cookies and strawberry cake. Then they suddenly changed their tune. No more nice, quiet, sedate, well-behaved little Teddy Bears! They ran and they romped and they chased. They laughed and they screamed and they hollered. Sometimes they bumped into each other and growled most terrible growls. "Gr-r-r-r, gr-r-r-r, gr-r-r-r!" It was something awful to hear.

But they quieted down at last and went home most politely. And all the Teddy Bears said they had had a wonderful time.

*In the music, you can hear the Teddy Bears march, growl, romp and play, then go home in perfect order.

The Gingerbread Man

A NEW ENGLAND TALE

ONCE upon a time there lived a little old woman and a little old man. They hadn't any little boys or girls of their own, so they lived in a little old house all alone. One day the little old woman was making gingerbread.

"I will make a little Gingerbread Boy," she said. So she rolled the dough out flat and cut it in the shape of a little boy. She put a row of currants down the front of his jacket for buttons. Then she made eyes of fat raisins, a mouth of pink sugar frosting, and a little peaked cap of white frosting. She pinched his gingerbread nose and ears into shape, and made two nice, good-sized feet.

THE GINGERBREAD MAN

"Hah! hah! Now we'll have a little Gingerbread Boy," laughed she.

She laid him flat on his back in the pan, popped him into the oven, and closed the door; then she went about her work, sweeping and cleaning the house—sweeping and cleaning, and she forgot all about the little Gingerbread Boy.

He baked, he got glossy brown all over, he got hot— very hot, and still the old woman swept and cleaned and cleaned and swept.

"Mercy!" said the little old woman at last, sniffing the air, "the Gingerbread Boy is burning."

She ran to the oven and opened the door, and up jumped the Gingerbread Boy. He hopped on the floor, ran across the kitchen, out of the door, down the walk, through the gate and down the road as fast as his gingerbread legs could carry him! The little old woman and the little old man ran after him, calling "Stop! Stop, little Gingerbread Boy!"

The Gingerbread Boy looked back and laughed and called out:

"Run! Run! Run!
Catch me if you can!
You can't get me!
I'm the Gingerbread Man,
I am! I am!"

And they couldn't catch him.

So the Gingerbread Boy ran on and on. Soon he came to a cow.

"Um! um!" sniffed the cow. "Stop, little Gingerbread Boy! I would like to eat you."

But the little Gingerbread Boy laughed and said:

"I've run away from a little old woman,
I've run away from a little old man,
And I can run away from you, I can."

So the cow ran after him.

THE GINGERBREAD MAN

But the Gingerbread Boy shouted back:

> "Run! Run! Run!
> Catch me if you can!
> You can't get me!
> I'm the Gingerbread Man,
> I am! I am!"

And the cow couldn't catch him.

So the little Gingerbread Boy ran on and on.

Soon he came to a horse.

"Please stop, little Gingerbread Boy," said the horse. "You look very good to eat."

But the little Gingerbread Boy called out:

> "I've run away from a little old woman,
> I've run away from a little old man,
> I've run away from a cow,
> And I can run away from you, I can."

So the horse ran after him.

When the little Gingerbread Boy was past, he looked back and called:

"Run! Run! Run!
Catch me if you can!
You can't get me!
I'm the Gingerbread Man,
I am! I am!"

And the horse couldn't catch him.

By and by the little Gingerbread Boy came to a barn where threshers were working.

The threshers saw the little Gingerbread Boy running and they tried to catch him and pick him up. They called to one another:

"Here is a gingerbread boy. Um! um! He smells good. Do not run so fast, little Gingerbread Boy. Gingerbread boys are made to eat."

But the little Gingerbread Boy ran faster and faster and called out:

"Ho! ho!
I've run away from a little old woman,
I've run away from a little old man,
I've run away from a cow,
I've run away from a horse,
And I can run away from you,
I can, I can!"

THE GINGERBREAD MAN

So the threshers ran after him.
But the Gingerbread Boy looked back and laughed:

> "Run! Run! Run!
> Catch me if you can!
> You can't get me!
> I'm the Gingerbread Man,
> I am! I am!"

And the threshers could not catch him.

Then the little Gingerbread Boy ran faster than ever. He ran and ran till he came to a field full of mowers. When the mowers saw how fine he looked, they ran after him calling:

"Wait a bit! Wait a bit, little Gingerbread Boy! Gingerbread boys are made to eat."

But the little Gingerbread Boy laughed harder than ever and ran like the wind. "Oh, ho! Oh, ho!" he cried,

> "I've run away from a little old woman,
> I've run away from a little old man,
> I've run away from a cow,
> I've run away from a horse,
> I've run away from a barn full of threshers,
> And I can run away from you,
> I can! I can!"

And the mowers couldn't catch him.

By this time the little Gingerbread Boy was very proud of himself. He strutted, he danced, he pranced! He thought no one on earth could catch him.

Pretty soon he saw a fox coming across a field. The fox looked at him and began to run, but the little Gingerbread Boy ran faster still and shouted out:

THE GINGERBREAD MAN

"Run! Run! Run!
Catch me if you can!
You can't get me!
I'm the Gingerbread Man,
I am! I am!
I've run away from a little old woman,
I've run away from a little old man,
I've run away from a cow,
I've run away from a horse,
I've run away from a barn full of threshers,
I've run away from a field full of mowers,
And I can run away from you,
I can! I can!"

"Why," said the fox politely, "I wouldn't catch you if I could."

Just then the little Gingerbread Boy came to a river. He dared not jump into the water he would have melted away, frosting cap and all, if he had . Still, the cow, the horse, and the people were chasing hot on his heels and he was forced to cross the river to keep out of their reach.

"Jump on my tail and I will take you across," said the fox. So the little Gingerbread Boy jumped on the fox's tail and the fox swam into the river. A little distance from the shore the fox said: "Little Gingerbread Boy,

I think you had better get on my back or you may fall off!"

So the little Gingerbread Boy jumped on the fox's back.

After swimming a little farther, the fox said:

"The water is deep. You may get wet where you are. Jump up on my shoulder."

So the little Gingerbread Boy jumped up on the fox's shoulder. When they were near the other side of the river the fox cried out suddenly:

"The water grows deeper still. Jump up on my nose! Jump up on my nose!"

So the little Gingerbread Boy jumped up on the fox's nose.

Then the fox sprang ashore and threw back his head. Snip, half the Gingerbread Boy was gone. Snip, snap, he was three-quarters gone and snip, snip, snap, at last, at last and at last that Gingerbread Boy went the way of every single gingerbread boy that ever came out of an oven! He was all, all gone!

Dawlish Fair

OVER the hill and over the dale
　　And over the Bourne to Dawlish,
Where gingerbread wives have a scanty sale,
And gingerbread nuts are smallish.

—*John Keats*

The Poor Old Lady*

THERE once was a poor old lady
  With nothing at all to eat
But cakes and fruits and sweetmeats,
Bread and fish and meat!

For drink she had only cocoa,
Chocolate, milk and tea,
Wine and soup and coffee;
Not one drop more had she!

And this very poor old lady
Had no place to live at all
Except for a house with a garden
An orchard and fine stone wall!

Not a soul took care of the lady
Save Andrew and John and Hugh,
Eight servants and two small pages
In livery of silver and blue!

*Translated from *La Pobre Viejecita* by Rafael Pombo, one of the favorite poets of Colombia, South America. *The Poor Old Lady* is as well-known to Colombian children as is Mother Goose to children in England and America.

She hadn't a thing to sit on
But sofas and chairs I'm told,
And no other bed but a big one
That shone like an altar with gold!

Whenever she looked in the glass,
She was always frightened to see
An old lady all dressed up in frills
With a wig where her hair ought to be!

For this very poor old lady
Had nothing at all to wear
But clothes of a thousand styles
Made of cloth that was costly and rare!

If it hadn't been for her boots,
Her shoes for the house and street,
Her slippers and overshoes,
She'd have walked on naked feet!

And this very poor old lady
When she died, I've heard,
Left nothing but gold and jewels
Six houses, eight cats, and a bird!

Come, Little Leaves*

GEORGE COOPER

"COME, little leaves," said the wind one day.
"Come over the meadows with me and play;
Put on your dresses of red and gold,
For summer is gone and the days grow cold."

Soon as the leaves heard the wind's loud call,
Down they came fluttering, one and all;
Over the brown fields they danced and flew,
Singing the sweet little songs they knew.

"Cricket, good-by, we've been friends so long,
Little brook, sing us your farewell song;
Say you are sorry to see us go;
Ah, you will miss us, right well we know."

Dancing and whirling, the little leaves went,
Winter had called them and they were content;
Soon, fast asleep in their earthy beds,
The snow laid a coverlid over their heads.

*The Whirlwind, written for the flute by Krantz, depicts a capricious whirlwind as it dances
through the air, tossing the leaves in a gay whirl.

The Little Rooster and the Little Hen

A CZECHOSLOVAKIAN FOLK TALE

ONCE on a time, a Little Rooster and a Little Hen went out in the woods to hunt for strawberries and they agreed to divide with each other all the fruit they found.

First, the Little Hen found a strawberry. "Cluck, cluck, cluck," she called and, when the Rooster came, she divided the berry with him.

By and by the Little Rooster, in his turn, found a strawberry; but he didn't call cluck, cluck. He gobbled the berry whole to get it all for himself, and the berry was so big, it stuck fast in his throat. Try as he would, he could not swallow it! He stretched out his neck, he shook his head, he jumped around on his two little legs, and then he fell flat on the ground choking and choking and choking.

The Little Hen came running to see how she could help him. Water was what he needed. So the Little Hen ran to the brook, and she cried, "O brook, good brook, please give me a drop of water for my little partner, the Rooster. He is lying flat on his back and choking and choking and choking."

All countries have the cumulative tales so loved by children, which gather together, link by link in rhythmical sequence, a chain of events. They go back to an old Chaldean hymn and to the Jewish Passover Liturgy.

But the brook said, "I will give you a drop of water when you bring me a leaf from the linden tree."

So the Little Hen ran to the linden tree and cried,

"O linden tree, good linden tree, please give me one of your leaves that I may give it to the brook, that the brook may give me some water for my little partner, the Rooster, who is lying flat on his back and choking and choking and choking."

But the linden tree said, "I will give you a leaf when you bring me a kerchief that the peasant woman is making."

So the Little Hen ran off to the peasant woman and she cried, "O woman, good woman, please give me a kerchicf that I may give it to the linden tree, that the linden tree may give me a leaf, that I may give it to the brook, that the brook may give me some water for my little partner, the Rooster, who is lying flat on his back and choking and choking and choking."

But the peasant woman said, "I will give you a kerchief when you bring me some silk from the Queen of Saba." So the Little Hen ran to the Queen and cried, "O Queen, please give me a bit of silk that I may give it to the woman that she may give me a kerchief, that I may give it to the linden tree, that the linden tree may give me a leaf, that I may give it to the brook, that the brook may give me some water for my little partner, the Rooster, who is lying flat on his back and choking and choking and choking."

But the Queen of Saba said, "I'll give you a piece of silk when you bring me a pair of shoes from the shoemaker." So the Little Hen ran to the shoemaker and cried, "O shoemaker, please give me a pair of shoes, that I may give them to the Queen, that she may give me a piece of silk, that I may give it to the woman, that she may give me a kerchief, that I may give it to the linden tree, that the tree may give me a leaf, that I may give it to the brook, that the brook may give me some water for my little partner, the Rooster, who is lying flat on his back, choking and choking and choking."

But the shoemaker said, "I'll give you a pair of shoes when you bring me some cream from the farmer's wife." So the Little Hen flew to the farmer's wife and cried, "O farmer's wife, please give me some cream, that I may give it to the shoemaker, that he may give me a pair of shoes, that I may give them to the Queen, that she may give me a bit of silk, that I may give it to the woman, that she may give me a kerchief, that I may give it to the linden tree, that the linden tree may give me a leaf, that I may give it to the brook, that the brook may give me some water for my little partner, the Rooster,

who is lying flat on his back and choking and choking and choking." But the farmer's wife said, "I will give you some cream when you bring me a bag full of grass."

Well, the Little Hen was all tired out. But still she ran off to the meadow and began to pluck the grass. She filled a whole bag full. Then she dragged the bag of grass away to the farmer's wife, and the farmer's wife gave her the cream.

So the Little Hen
gave the cream to the
shoemaker who gave her a pair of shoes.
And she took the shoes to the Queen of Saba who gave her
a bit of silk. And she took the bit of silk to the peasant woman
who gave her a kerchief. And she took the kerchief to the linden
tree who gave her a leaf. And she took the leaf to the brook. And
then and there, the brook gave her that drop of water!

The Little Hen hurried back to the place where she
had left the Little Rooster. He was choking so at that moment he could
hardly get his breath. But the Little Hen dropped the water into his
beak and the water ran down his throat and washed that big strawberry
down. Then the Little Rooster jumped up and flapped his wings for joy.

"Cock-a-doodle-do!" he cried. But after that, when the Little Rooster
found something good to eat, he divided with the Little Hen.

Laughing Song

WILLIAM BLAKE

WHEN the meadows laugh with lively green,
  And the grasshopper laughs in the merry scene;
When Mary, and Susan, and Emily
With their sweet round mouths sing, "Ha, Ha, He!"

When the painted birds laugh in the shade,
Where our table with cherries and nuts is spread:
Come live, and be merry, and join with me,
To sing the sweet chorus of "Ha, Ha, He!"

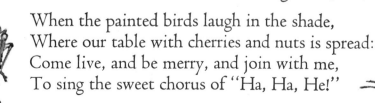

Grasshopper Green

GRASSHOPPER GREEN is a comical chap;
He lives on the best of fare.
Bright little trousers, jacket, and cap—
These are his summer wear.
Out in the meadow he loves to go,
Playing away in the sun;
It's hopperty, skipperty, high and low—
Summer's the time for fun.

Grasshopper Green has a dozen wee boys,
And, soon as their legs grow strong,
Each of them joins in his frolicsome joys,
Singing his merry song.

Under the hedge in a happy row,
Soon as the day has begun,
It's hopperty, skipperty, high and low—
Summer's the time for fun.

Grasshopper Green has a quaint little house.
It's under the hedge so gay.
Grandmother Spider, as still as a mouse,
Watches him over the way.
Gladly he's calling the children, I know,
Out in the beautiful sun;
It's hopperty, skipperty, high and low—
Summer's the time for fun.

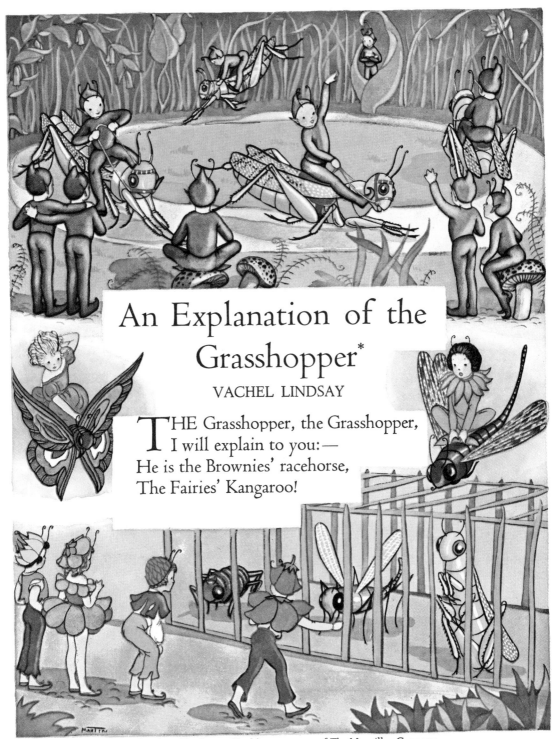

An Explanation of the Grasshopper*

VACHEL LINDSAY

THE Grasshopper, the Grasshopper,
  I will explain to you:—
He is the Brownies' racehorse,
The Fairies' Kangaroo!

*Taken from *The Congo*. Used by permission of The Macmillan Company.

Poems by Christina Rossetti

MINNIE and Mattie
 And fat little May,
Out in the country,
 Spending a day.

Pinky white pigling
 Squeals through his snout,
Woolly white lambkin
 Frisks all about.

A WHITE hen sitting
 On white eggs three:
Next, three speckled chickens
As plump as plump can be.

From *Sing Song* by Christina Rossetti. By permission of The Macmillan Company, publishers.

MIX a pancake,
Stir a pancake,
Pop it in the pan;
Fry the pancake,
Toss the pancake,
Catch it if you can.

LIE a-bed,
Sleepy head,
Shut up eyes, bo-peep;
Till day-break
Never wake:
Baby, sleep.

O SAILOR, come ashore,
What have you brought for me?
Red coral, white coral,
Coral from the sea.

A woman who always delighted in the simple joys of children was Christina Rossetti (English, 1830-1894), the author of *Sing Song*. She was a sister of the poet and painter, Dante Gabriel Rossetti, and often sat as a model for him while he painted.

A Song for Easter

OLIVE BEAUPRÉ MILLER

WAKE! Wake up you sleepers;
   Wake up sleeping earth;
Now is come the Easter,
Time for your rebirth!

All through snows of winter
You've been fast asleep!
Sunshine now is calling;
Little rabbits leap!

You, you little chickens,
In your eggs fast curled,
Peck out to the sunshine;
See the great big world!

You, you little seedlings,
Sleeping in the ground,
Send up shoots and blossoms;
Earth is green around.

Lambs and calves, come frisking!
All you young things play!
Life again is waking,
This is Easter day.

Ring the bells for Easter
Ring them full and deep!
It's Easter! Life's awaking
After winter's sleep!

The dainty *Spring Song* by Mendelssohn has all the lilt and dancing gaiety of spring. *Melody in F* by Rubinstein, sung with the words, "Sing then ye birds," expresses the more solemn gratitude of the Russian in the freshness of spring after Russia's long winter.

Whisky Frisky

WHISKY Frisky,
Hippity-hop,
Up he goes
To the tree top!

Whirly, twirly,
Round and round,
Down he scampers
To the ground.

Furly, curly,
What a tail!
Tall as a feather,
Broad as a sail!

Where's his supper?
In the shell;
Snappy, cracky,
Out it fell.

82

The Star

JANE TAYLOR

TWINKLE, twinkle, little star,
How I wonder what you are,
Up above the world, so high,
Like a diamond in the sky!

When the blazing sun is gone,
When he nothing shines upon,
Then you show your little light,
Twinkle, twinkle, all the night.

In the dark blue sky you keep,
And often through my curtains peep,
For you never shut your eye
Till the sun is in the sky.

And your bright and tiny spark
Lights the traveler in the dark;
Though I know not what you are,
Twinkle, twinkle, little star.

The City Mouse and
the Country Mouse
ADAPTED FROM AESOP

ONCE upon a time, there was
one little Mouse who lived
in the country and there was an-
other little Mouse who lived in the city. The Country Mouse
was very poor; he lived in a hole in the ground and had to
work very hard, but the City Mouse was very rich and he
lived in the pantry of a great big city house. Well, one day,
the City Mouse, all dressed in his best city clothes, came to
visit the Country Mouse in his poor little hole in the field.

"Why, my dear friend," said the City Mouse, seeing how
the Country Mouse lived. "How very poor you are!"

"Yes, I suppose I'm poor," said the little Country Mouse.
"I haven't much to offer a friend; but, if you'll make yourself comfortable, I'll get you something to eat."

So the City Mouse lay down lazily while the Country
Mouse went away and worked hard in the fields, digging up

roots and wheat-stalks. By and by he came home, very tired from his work but happy and proud of the dinner he was bringing home to his friend.

"Is that all you have to eat?" The City Mouse turned up his nose. "All this hard work in the fields and nothing to show for your labor but a few poor roots and wheat-stalks! You should see how I live in the city—all the finest food to be had, and for no work at all. The Cook in the house bakes the cake and, when she is out of the way, I sneak out and help myself! Thus she does all the work and I have all the fun. Come up to town and see!"

And now the Country Mouse was very sorry for himself. "I do work hard," he said, "and I get little in return. It must be fine not to work! I'll go up to town with you!"

So the two Mice walked back to town till they came to the grandest home the Country Mouse had ever seen, where they scampered into the pantry.

"This is like real living," said the City Mouse very proudly. "Look at those goodies on the shelf. We'll make a meal off that chocolate cake!"

They were creeping up to the cake, when bang! the kitchen door opened and there appeared the face of the Cook.

"Scat!" she cried and the Mice in a panic ran off to a hole.

"We'll have another chance in a moment," the City Mouse managed to squeak; but, when they crept out again, the Cook dashed in at once and chased them with a broom.

"Have a little patience, my friend. We'll get what we want in a moment," the City Mouse said, breathing hard.

So they waited a long, long time till they thought the Cook had forgotten them and then they came out again, very, very hungry now after their long walk to town. But, just as they started to nibble, the Cook pushed open the door and shoved in their most dreaded foe, Dame Pussy Cat herself!

"Mice in here!" she cried. "Catch them for me, Pussy!"

Off scampered the Mice in a jiffy, their hearts beating fast with fright, and as they crouched in the hole, hungry and terrified, Dame Pussy came and sat down, watching beside their hole and ready to spring in a moment if they should so much as show even the tips of their noses. Then the Country Mouse said to the City Mouse:

"Your life of ease, my friend, is not so fine as it sounds; for, though you do not work, neither are you certain of eating. I'd far rather work and know that I also shall eat!" And off he ran back home by ways out of reach of the Cat.

The Little Rabbit Who Wanted Red Wings

An American folktale retold by

CAROLYN SHERWIN BAILEY

ONCE upon a time, there was a little White Rabbit with two beautiful, long pink ears and two bright, red eyes and four soft, little feet—*such* a pretty little White Rabbit, but he wasn't happy.

Just think, this little White Rabbit wanted to be somebody else instead of the nice little rabbit that he was.

When Mr. Bushy Tail, the gray squirrel, went by, the little White Rabbit would say to his Mammy: "Oh, Mammy, I *wish* I had a long, gray tail like Mr. Bushy Tail's."

And when Mr. Porcupine went by, the little White Rabbit would say to his Mammy: "Oh, Mammy, I *wish* I had a back full of bristles like Mr. Porcupine's."

And when Miss Puddle-Duck went by in her two little red rubbers, the little White Rabbit would say: "Oh, Mammy, I *wish* I had a pair of red rubbers like Miss Puddle-Duck's."

From *For the Story Teller*. Used by the kind permission of the publishers, Milton Bradley Company.

So he went on and on wishing until his Mammy was clean tired out with his wishing and Old Mr. Ground Hog heard him one day. Old Mr. Ground Hog is very wise, so he said to the little White Rabbit: "Why don't you-all go down to the Wishing Pond, and, if you look in the water at yourself and turn around three times in a circle, you-all will get your wish."

So the little White Rabbit trotted off, all alone by himself through the woods until he came to a little pool of green water, and that was the Wishing Pond. There was a little, *little* bird, all red, sitting on the edge of the Wishing Pond to get a drink, and, as soon as the little White Rabbit saw him he began to wish again:

"Oh, I *wish* I had a pair of little red wings!" he said. Just then he looked in the Wishing Pond and he saw his little white face. Then he turned around three times and something happened. He began to have a queer feeling in his shoulders, like that he felt in his mouth when he was cutting his teeth. It was his wings coming through. So he sat all day in the woods by the Wishing Pond waiting for them to grow, and, by and by, when it was almost sundown, he started

home to see his Mammy and show her, because he had a beautiful pair of long, trailing red wings.

But by the time he reached home it was getting dark, and when he went in the hole at the foot of a big tree where he lived, his Mammy didn't know him. No, she really and truly did not know him, because, you see, she had never seen a rabbit with red wings in all her life. And so the little White Rabbit had to go out again, because his Mammy wouldn't let him get into his own bed. He had to go out and look for some place to sleep all night.

He went and went until he came to Mr. Bushy Tail's house, and he rapped on the door and said: "Please, kind Mr. Bushy Tail, may I sleep in your house all night?"

But Mr. Bushy Tail opened his door a crack and then he slammed it tight shut again. You see he had never seen a rabbit with red wings in all his life.

So the little White Rabbit went and went until he came to Miss Puddle-Duck's nest down by the marsh and he said: "Please, kind Miss Puddle-Duck, may I sleep in your nest all night?"

But Miss Puddle-Duck poked her head up out of her nest just a little way and then she shut her eyes and stretched her wings out so far that she covered her whole nest! You see she had never seen a rabbit with red wings in all her life.

So the little White Rabbit went and went until he came to Old Mr. Ground Hog's hole, and Old Mr. Ground Hog let him sleep with him all night, but the hole had beechnuts spread all over it. Old Mr. Ground Hog liked them to sleep on but they hurt the little White Rabbit's feet and made him very uncomfortable before morning.

THE LITTLE RABBIT

When it came morning, the little White Rabbit decided to try his wings and fly a little, so he climbed up on a hill and spread his wings and sailed off, but he landed in a low bush all full of prickles, and his four feet got mixed up with the twigs so he couldn't get down.

"Mammy, Mammy, Mammy, come and help me!" he called.

His Mammy didn't hear him, but Old Mr. Ground Hog did, and he came and helped the little White Rabbit out of the prickly bush.

"Don't you-all want your red wings?" Mr. Ground Hog asked.

"No, *no!*" said the little White Rabbit.

"Well," said the Old Ground Hog, "why don't you-all go down to the Wishing Pond and wish them off again?"

So the little White Rabbit went down to the Wishing Pond and he saw his face in it. Then he turned around three times, and, sure enough, his red wings were gone. Then he went home to his Mammy, who knew him right away and was so glad to see him, and he never, *never*, wished to be something different from what he really was again.

The Dancing Monkeys

ADAPTED FROM AESOP

ONCE upon a time a prince had some monkeys. They were very bright, funny little monkeys and so he taught them to dance. Heel-toe, forward and back! Soon they were able to dance for all the world like men and women. So the prince gave the monkeys fine clothes and he put them up on a stage to dance for all his friends. Night after night they danced just like real people.

By and by those who watched them began to say to each other: "Well, well, these must be men! We thought at first they were monkeys but surely they must be men!"

And the monkeys, too, began to think they were part of the tribe of men and to hold their heads very high.

"We're just as good as men!" they said to one another.

But, one day, a mischievous boy thought up a little trick.

THE DANCING MONKEYS

He threw some nuts on the stage as the monkeys were lined up to dance. Suddenly, at sight of the nuts, those monkeys forgot they were dancers; they forgot they had called themselves men. Breaking the line of their dance, they thought only of scrambling for nuts. Fighting with one another, they kicked and bit and chattered. And none of them was willing that any other monkey should get a single nut. That was a tussle for you! They tore all the clothes off each other. And now what a how-do-you-do! As they stood there without any clothes, everyone who was watching could see they were not really men. They were nothing at all but monkeys!

The people roared with laughter, while an old man cried from the crowd: "He, who thinks himself a man, will have to act like a man. Squabbling, you show yourselves monkeys! Fighting, you show yourselves beasts!"

Ten Little Indians

TEN little Indians
    standing in a line—
One went home
    and then there were nine.

Nine little Indians
        swinging on a gate—
One jumped off
        and then there were eight.

Eight little Indians
        staying at a tavern—
One went away
        and then there were seven.

Seven little Indians
        playing pretty tricks—
One went to ride
        and then there were six.

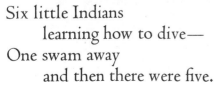

Six little Indians
        learning how to dive—
One swam away
        and then there were five.

Five little Indians
    peeped through the door—
One ran behind
    and then there were four.

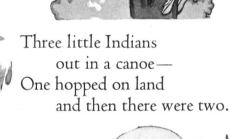

Four little Indians
    climbed up a tree—
One slid down
    and then there were three.

Three little Indians
    out in a canoe—
One hopped on land
    and then there were two.

Two little Indians
    playing in the sun—
One fell asleep
    and then there was one.

One little Indian
    playing all alone—
He went in the house
    and then there was none.

MATILDA BREUER

The Foolish, Timid, Little Hare

AN EAST INDIAN FABLE

ONCE there was a foolish, timid, little Hare, who was always expecting something awful to happen. She was forever saying, "Suppose the earth were to crack and swallow me up!" She said this over and over again till at last she really believed the earth was about to crack and swallow her up.

One day she was asleep under a palm tree when some Monkeys above dropped a cocoanut down. The little Hare didn't see the cocoanut, but she heard its thud on the ground. Up she jumped in a hurry and cried: "Dear me! The earth is surely cracking!" And she ran away as fast as she could, without ever looking behind her.

Presently she met an older Hare, who called out after her, "Why are you running so fast?"

The foolish, timid, little Hare answered, "The earth is cracking and I'm running away, so as not to be swallowed up!"

"Is that it?" cried the second Hare. "Dear me! Then I'll run away too!" and off he dashed beside her. Soon they met another Hare; they told him the earth was cracking, and off he dashed beside them. So it went on, till at last there were a hundred-thousand Hares all running away as fast as they could.

By and by the Hares met a Deer. "Why are you all running so fast?" asked the Deer.

"The earth is cracking!" they wailed. "We're running away so as not to be swallowed up!"

"The earth is cracking? Oh, dear me!" cried the Deer, and she bounded after the crowd as fast as she could go.

A little farther on, they passed a Tiger.

"Why are you all running so fast?" called the Tiger.

"The earth is cracking!" the fearful ones wailed. "And we're running away so as not to be swallowed up!"

"The earth is cracking? Oh, dear me!" howled the Tiger, and he leapt away after the crowd as fast as he could go.

In a few minutes more, they met an Elephant.

"Why are you all running so fast?" asked the Elephant.

"The earth is cracking!" the fearful ones wailed. "And we're running away so as not to be swallowed up!"

"The earth is cracking? Oh, dear me!" trumpeted the Elephant, and he lumbered off after the crowd as fast as he could go.

At last the wise King Lion saw the animals running

pell-mell, head over heels in a crazy crowd, and he heard them cry, "The earth is cracking!" Then he ran out boldly before them and roared three times till they halted.

"What is this you are saying?" he cried.

"Oh, King!" they answered. "The earth is cracking! We'll all be swallowed up!"

"Hoity-toity!" roared King Lion. "Let's take time to find out if such a thing could be true. Who was it that saw the earth crack?"

"Not I," said the Elephant. "Ask the Tiger! He told me!"

"Not I," said the Tiger. "Ask the Deer! She told me!"

"Not I," said the Deer. "Ask the Hares! They told me!"

So every single animal said he had not been the one to see the earth crack and he pointed out someone else who

had told him all about it. When it came to the Hares, they pointed to the one foolish, timid, little Hare, who stood by shivering and shaking. "She told us," they all cried.

Then the Lion said, "Little Hare, what made you say the earth was cracking?"

"I heard it crack," said the Hare.

"Where did you hear it crack?" asked the Lion.

"By the big palm tree. I was fast asleep, and I woke up and thought, 'Oh, dear me! Suppose the earth should crack and swallow me up!' Just then I heard a cracking noise, as loud—as loud as thunder—and away I ran as fast as I could."

"Well," said the Lion, "you and I will go back to the place where the earth is cracking and see what is the matter."

"No, no, no!" cried the foolish, timid, little Hare. "I would not go there again for anything in the world."

"But," said the Lion, "I will take you on my back." So at last the foolish, timid, little Hare got up on the Lion's back and away they went like the wind, till they came to the Palm Tree. No sooner had they arrived than they heard a loud thud—the Monkeys threw down another cocoanut! And there they had the secret at last! At last the Hare understood how nothing but a falling cocoanut had made her think the earth was cracking. So the foolish, timid, little Hare went back to the other animals and said, "The earth is *not* cracking."

"Well! Well! Well!" said the Elephant. "You don't say! So the earth is *not* cracking after all!" And he lumbered off into the forest.

Thus every one of the animals went back into the forest, and that was the end of the earthquake.

Noah's Ark

RETOLD FROM THE BIBLE

IN the beginning God made everybody and told them all to be good. But by-and-by everybody began to be very bad. Then God said:

"Always I tell My people how to be good. But they don't listen to Me any more. They're very bad. So I'll have to send a flood of waters to wash the earth clean of these bad people."

But there was one man in the world who was good. His name was Noah. And because Noah was good, God wanted to save him from being washed away with the others. So God said to Noah:

"Noah, soon waters will cover the earth. Build for yourself and your family a boat, a big boat, an ark that will float on the waters."

And Noah listened to God as he always did. He and his wife and his sons and his sons' wives worked very hard to build the ark. But the other people didn't listen to God, so they didn't hear a word God said about the flood of waters and how they could save themselves from it. They just played around and were as bad to each other as ever. Then God said to Noah:

"Take into the ark two of every kind of creature and go into the ark yourself with your wife and your sons and your sons' wives."

So Noah took into the ark two of every kind of bird and animal—cattle and giraffes and pigs and lions and all the rest. And after them Noah and his family also went into the ark.

Then it started to rain. It rained and rained for forty days and forty nights till the water covered the earth and washed the bad people away. But all those that were with Noah stayed alive, snug and cozy in the ark.

At last God told the rain to stop and the ark stopped floating around. It came to rest on a big, tall mountain top. Then Noah opened a window and looked out. But all he could see was water, water, water, with just a few mountain tops showing above it. So he sent forth a raven and a dove to fly over the earth and see if there was any place where the water had gone down and left dry land. But the dove flew back to Noah and he knew she had found no dry land or she would have stayed there. So he waited seven days more. Then he sent the dove out again. In the evening she flew back to him with the leaf from an olive tree in her beak. And because she had found that leaf, Noah knew that the waters had now sunk down below the treetops. So he waited seven days more. Then he sent the dove out again. This time she never came back. So Noah knew she had found dry land to live on and that the waters were gone from the earth.

Then God told Noah to take his wife and his sons and his sons' wives and every other living thing out of the ark. So they all went out on dry land—people and lions and lambs and tigers and cattle and monkeys and dogs and all the rest. They were all very happy together. And Noah gave thanks to God because He had saved them from the flood of waters. Then the sun came shining through the clouds and Noah and his family saw hanging in the sky a beautiful shining thing, a bow of many colors that went soaring like a bridge between the earth and the sky. And they heard God saying to them:

"This is the rainbow. I have set it in the sky as the sign of a promise I make you. Whenever you see the rainbow shining out of the clouds, remember that I promise always to keep my good people safe. Never again will I let the waters come as a flood to cover the earth."

The Bow
That Bridges Heaven

CHRISTINA G. ROSSETTI

BOATS sail on the rivers,
  And ships sail on the seas,
But clouds that sail across the skies
Are prettier than these.
There are bridges in the river,
As pretty as you please,
But the bow that bridges heaven
And overtops the trees,
And builds a roof from earth to sky
Is prettier far than these.

The Hare and the Tortoise

ADAPTED FROM AESOP

A HARE once said boastfully that he could run faster than any of the other little forest creatures.

"I have never been beaten and never shall be!" said he. 'I dare anyone to race with me."

The Tortoise answered quietly: "I will race with you."

"You!" laughed the Hare. "Hah! Hah! A Turtle run a race with a Hare! You slow-poke, I could dance around you every inch of the way and still reach the goal ahead of you!"

"Keep such big talk as that until you've won the race!" That's what the Tortoise answered.

Well, all the little Forest Folk came to see the fun.

"Friend Turtle, whose legs are so short that he can hardly crawl, will run a race with the Hare!" Woodchuck chuckled. "Why, the Hare's hind legs are so long he can go at one leap as far as Friend Turtle can go in fifty slow creeping steps!" Then all the little Forest Folk laughed. But the Tortoise still stuck to it that he would run the race.

106

THE HARE AND THE TORTOISE

So the Hare and the Tortoise went
and put their toes to the starting line.
"Make ready!" cried the Raccoon.
"One, two, three, go!" They were off!

The Hare darted almost out of sight, leaping enormous
leaps, but, when he had gone half-way, what did he do but
stop. He would show that old slow-poke what he thought of

 his racing! He lay down and went to sleep,
so certain was he of reaching the goal
ahead of the Tortoise. He slept and he
slept and he slept, but the Tortoise plodded on; he plodded on, and plodded on.

At last the Hare woke up. Good gracious, what did he see!
The Tortoise had gone all around the course mapped out for
the race. He was back near the winning-post! The Hare gave
a great big leap. He ran as fast as he could to make up for the
time he had lost, but he could not catch up with the Tortoise.
The Tortoise crawled over the goal a full length ahead of the
Hare. "Three cheers for Friend Turtle!" shouted the Forest
People. But the Tor-
toise said to the Hare:
"He, who keeps stead-
ily at work, always
comes out ahead."

The Lion and the Mouse

ADAPTED FROM AESOP

ONCE a great big Lion lay fast asleep in the woods. By-and-by a Mouse came along, a little teeny, tiny Mouse. Now the Lion was lying so still, the Mouse thought he was only a big heap of dried brown grass. So the Mouse began scampering around up and down on the Lion's body.

Pretty soon—"Gr!" growled the Lion. The little feet of the Mouse were tickling the Lion's stomach. Tickle, tickle, tickle, went the Mouse. The Lion squirmed and he grunted. He opened one big, round eye and then he opened the other. He saw the teeny, tiny Mouse and he woke up wide awake! He reached out a paw and snap! He snatched the little Mouse.

"So, it's you!" he roared. "It's you who've awakened me! I'll just put a stop to that! I'll eat you for my breakfast!"

Well, the Mouse was terribly frightened. His heart went

pit-a-pat, but he squeaked in a little bit of voice: "O mighty King of the Beasts, please don't eat me up! I'll never forget your kindness if you'll let me go this once!"

But the Lion opened his jaws. He opened his great big mouth and began to smack his lips. "Yum, yum, little Mouse," he said. "I think you will taste very good!"

Trembling all over, the Mouse began to coax harder and harder: "Please let me go! O please! Who knows, great King of the Beasts, if you would let me go, it might even happen some day that I could be helpful to you!"

"You help me!" cried the Lion. "A teeny, tiny thing like you help the great big King of the Beasts. Hah hah! Haw haw! Ho ho!" He laughed so loud and so long that all the forest rang. But he laughed so loud and so long that he made himself feel very jolly. "Well, after all," he said, "you're really far too small to be even one bite for me. I'll catch something better for breakfast!" And he opened his great, big paw so the little Mouse slipped out and scampered as fast as he could to hide himself in the grass.

Well, not long after this, the Lion was wandering in the

woods when he suddenly fell in a hole that had been dug by some hunters who wanted to catch the Lion. These hunters meant to put the Lion in a cage and carry him to their King. They meant to set the cage for a show in the palace yard so the people might come and see this beautiful, great, big beast.

The Lion was groaning in the hole when the band of hunters found him. They drew him up out of the trap and tied him with a rope to a tree. Then they went off and left him in order to get a wagon to carry him to the palace.

"I must get away," thought the Lion, "before the hunters come back!" And he tugged and tore at the rope but he could not get himself free. And so at last he cried sadly: "They have me! I cannot get loose! I shall end my life in a cage. Nevermore shall I see this great, big, beautiful forest!"

But as he was crying and sighing, it chanced that the Mouse came by, the teeny, tiny little Mouse.

"Well, well, friend Lion," he squeaked. "What's this that has happened to you, the great big King of the Beasts?"

"The hunters have bound me fast," the Lion groaned. "There isn't a thing I can do to break this great, strong rope."

"Is that all the trouble, friend?" the Mouse laughed cheerily.

"You needn't seem so glad about it. It's a very sad end for me!" the Lion began to grumble.

But already the little Mouse had gone straight up to the

rope and begun with his sharp teeth to gnaw it. He gnawed and he gnawed and he gnawed. And pretty soon split, split, split, the rope began to break. Then he gnawed and he gnawed some more. Split, split, split, went the rope. Bit by bit, the Mouse chewed until all at once—snip, snap, he had gnawed through the very last strand. The rope broke straight in two and there stood the Lion free!

"You thought I could never help you," the Little Mouse squeaked to the Lion, "but look, I have set you free!"

"Well, well!" The Lion was so surprised he could hardly speak. "Just look at what you've done! A teeny, tiny thing like you to set free the King of the Forest! I'm ashamed that I laughed at you. You've shown me that, no matter how very small one is, he can always be helpful to others, although they are larger than he. Goodbye, little friend! I thank you!" And the Lion ran with a bound off into the forest.

THE SONG OF SOLOMON

LO, the winter is past;
the rain is over and gone;
The flowers appear on the earth;
the time of the singing of birds is come.

—*The Bible.*

Oeyvind and Marit

(A Story of Norway)

BJÖRNSTJERNE BJÖRNSON

OEYVIND was his name. A low, rocky cliff overhung the house where he was born, fir and birch trees looked down upon the roof, and the wild cherry strewed flowers over it. On this roof lived a little goat belonging to Oeyvind; it was kept there that it might not wander away, and Oeyvind carried leaves and grass up to it.

From *The Happy Boy*. By permission of Houghton Mifflin Co. In Norway the peasants often covered their roofs with squares of turf in which grass continued to grow and from which even small bushes sometimes sprouted; good pasturage for a goat.

One fine day, the goat leaped down and ran off to the cliff; it went straight up and soon stood where it had never been before. Oeyvind did not see the goat when he came out in the afternoon and thought at once of the fox. He grew hot all over, looked round about, and called: "Here, goat! Here, goat! Here, goat!"

"Ba-a-a!" answered the goat from the top of the hill, putting its head on one side and looking down. At the side of the goat, there was kneeling a little girl.

"Is this goat yours?" asked she.

Oeyvind opened wide his mouth and eyes, thrust both hands into his breeches and said, "Who are you?"

"I am Marit, mother's little one, father's fiddle, the elf in the house, granddaughter to Ola Nordistuen of the Heide farms, four years old in the autumn—I am!"

"Is that who you are?" cried he, drawing a long breath, for he had not dared to take one while she was speaking.

"Is this goat yours?" she asked again.

"Ye-es!" replied he.

"I like it so very much. Will you not give it to me?"

"No indeed, I will not!"

She lay flat on the ground staring down at him, and soon she said: "But if I give you a twisted bun for the goat, may I have it then?"

Oeyvind was the son of poor people; he had tasted twisted bun only once in his life, that was when grandfather came to his house and he had never eaten anything so good before or since. He fixed his eyes on the girl.

OEYVIND AND MARIT

"Let me see the bun first," said he.

She was not long in showing him a
large twisted bun that she held in her hand.

"Here it is!" cried she, and tossed it to him.

"Oh, it broke in pieces!" said the boy,
picking up every bit with the greatest care.
He could not help tasting the very
smallest morsel, and it was so good
that he had to try another, till before
he knew it, he had eaten up the whole bun.

"Now the goat belongs to me," said the girl.

The boy stopped with the last bit in his mouth. The
girl lay there laughing, and the goat stood by her side,
looking sideways down.

"Could you not wait a while?" begged the boy, his
heart beginning to beat fast. The girl laughed more than
ever and quickly got up on her knees.

"No, the goat is mine," said she and threw her arms
about it. Then, loosening one of her garters, she fastened
it about its neck. Oeyvind watched her. She rose to her
feet and began to tug at the goat; it would not go along
with her, and stretched its neck over the edge of the cliff
toward Oeyvind. "Ba-a-a-a!" said the goat.

Then the little girl took hold of its hair with one hand, pulled at the garter with the other, and said prettily: "Come now, goat, you shall go into the sitting-room and eat from mother's dish." And off she went.

There the boy stood. He had taken care of the goat ever since winter, when it was born, and he had never dreamed that he could lose it; but now it was gone in a moment and he would never see it again.

His mother came up humming from the beach, with some wooden pails she had been scouring. She saw the boy sitting on the grass, with his legs crossed under him, crying, and she went to him.

"What makes you cry?"

"Oh, my goat—my goat!"

"Why, where is the goat?" asked the mother, looking up at the roof.

"It will never come back anymore," said the boy.

"Dear me! How can that be?"

Oeyvind would not tell what he had done at first.

"Has the fox carried it off?"

"Oh, I wish it were the fox."

"Then, what has become of it?" cried the mother.

"Oh — oh — oh! I happened to — to — to sell it for a twisted bun!"

As soon as he spoke, the boy understood what he had done, to sell his pet goat for a bun; he had not thought about it before.

The mother said, "What do you suppose the goat thinks of you, when you're willing to sell it for a twisted bun?"

The boy thought this over and felt perfectly sure that he could never be happy again. He was so sorry for what he had done, that he promised himself he would never do anything wrong again—neither cut the cord of the spinning wheel, nor let the sheep loose, nor go down to the sea alone. He fell asleep and dreamed about his goat. Then something wet was thrust right against his ear and he started up. "Ba-a-a-a!" he heard, and it was the goat that had returned to him.

"What! Have you come back again?" He sprang up, seized it by the two forelegs, and danced about with it as if it were a brother. He pulled it by the beard and was on the point of going in to his mother with it, when he heard someone behind him, and saw the little girl sitting on the grass. Now he understood why the goat had come back and he let go of it.

"Is it you who have brought the goat?"

She sat tearing up the grass with her hands and said, "I was not allowed to keep it; grandfather is up there waiting." While the boy stood staring at her, a sharp voice from the road above called, "Well!"

Then she remembered what she had been told to do; she rose, walked up to Oeyvind, thrust one of her dirt-covered hands into his, and turning her face away said, "I beg your pardon!" But then her courage was all gone; she flung her arms about the goat and burst into tears.

"I believe you had better keep the goat," stammered Oeyvind, looking the other way.

"Make haste now!" called her grandfather from the hill, so Marit turned and walked slowly toward him.

"You have forgotten your garter," Oeyvind shouted after her. She turned and looked at him, then she answered in a choked voice, "You may keep it." He walked up to her, took her hand and said, "I thank you."

"Oh, it's nothing to thank for," she answered, but she still sobbed as she walked away.

Oeyvind sat down on the grass again, the goat roaming about near him, but he was no longer as happy with it as before.

The same summer his mother began to teach him to read. Then, one day, she said to him, "Tomorrow school begins again and you are going."

Oeyvind had heard that school was a place where boys played together and he was greatly pleased. He walked faster than his mother up the hillside, so eager was he. When they came to the schoolhouse, a loud buzzing like that from the mill at home, met them and he asked his mother what it was.

"It is the children reading," answered she.

On entering, he saw many children around a table; others sat on their dinner pails along the wall, some stood in groups around a large printed card covered with numbers. The schoolmaster, an old gray-haired man, sat on a stool by the chimney corner.

They all looked up as Oeyvind and his mother came in and the mill-hum ceased as if the water had been suddenly turned off. The mother bowed to the schoolmaster, who returned her greeting.

"I have come here to bring a little boy who wants to learn to read," said the mother.

"What is his name?" asked the schoolmaster.

"Oeyvind. He knows his letters and he can spell."

"You don't say so," said the schoolmaster. "Come here, little Whitehead."

Oeyvind went over to him; the schoolmaster took him on his lap and raised his cap.

"What a nice little boy!" said he and stroked his hair. Oeyvind looked up into his eyes and laughed.

"Is it at me you are laughing?" asked the schoolmaster with a frown.

"Yes, it is," answered Oeyvind, and roared with laughter. At that the schoolmaster laughed; Oeyvind's mother laughed; the children understood that they also might laugh, and so they all laughed together.

OEYVIND AND MARIT

When Oeyvind was to take his seat, all the scholars wished to make room for him. He, on his part, looked about for a long time. Then he spied near the hearth-stone, close beside him, sitting on a little red-painted box, Marit with the many names. She had hidden her face behind both hands and sat peeping out at him.

"I will sit here!" cried Oeyvind at once, and, seizing a lunchbox, he seated himself at her side. Now she raised the arm nearest him a little and peered at him from under her elbow; forthwith he, too, covered his face with both hands and looked at her from under his elbow. Thus they sat cutting capers till the reading began again! The children read aloud, each from his book, high little voices piping up and lower voices drumming, while here and there one chimed in to be heard above all the rest. In his whole life, Oeyvind had never had such fun.

"Is it always like this here?" he whispered to Marit.

"Yes, always," said she.

Later, they too had to go for-
ward to the schoolmaster to
read; then they were allowed
to sit quietly down again.

"I have a goat now myself,"
said Marit.

"Have you?" cried Oeyvind,
and that was the very best
thing he learned on his first
day at school.

Over in the Meadow

OLIVE A. WADSWORTH

OVER in the meadow,
   In the sand, in the sun,
Lived an old mother-toad
   And her little toadie one.
"Wink," said the mother;
   "I wink," said the one;
So she winked and she blinked
   In the sand, in the sun.

Over in the meadow,
   Where the stream runs blue,
Lived an old mother-fish
   And her little fishes two.
"Swim," said the mother;
   "We swim," said the two;
So they swam and they leaped
   Where the stream runs blue.

Over in the meadow,
    In a hole in a tree,
Lived an old mother-bluebird
    And her little birdies three.
"Sing," said the mother;
    "We sing," said the three;
So they sang and were glad,
    In the hole in the tree.

Over in the meadow,
    In the reeds on the shore,
Lived a mother-muskrat
    And her little ratties four.
"Dive," said the mother;
    "We dive," said the four;
So they dived and they burrowed
    In the reeds on the shore.

DONN P. CRANE

Over in the meadow,
　　In a snug bee-hive,
Lived a mother honey-bee
　　And her little bees five.
"Buzz," said the mother;
　　"We buzz," said the five;
So they buzzed and they hummed
　　In the snug bee-hive.

Over in the meadow,
　　In a nest built of sticks,
Lived a black mother-crow
　　And her little crows six.
"Caw," said the mother;
　　"We caw," said the six;
So they cawed and they called
　　In their nest built of sticks.

Over in the meadow,
　　Where the grass is so even,
Lived a gay mother-cricket
　　And her little crickets seven.
"Chirp," said the mother;
　　"We chirp," said the seven;
So they chirped cheery notes
　　In the grass soft and even.

Over in the meadow,
    By the old mossy gate,
Lived a brown mother-lizard
    And her little lizards eight.
"Bask," said the mother;
    "We bask," said the eight;
So they basked in the sun
    On the old mossy gate.

Over in the meadow,
    Where the quiet pools shine,
Lived a green mother-frog
    And her little froggies nine.
"Croak," said the mother,
    "We croak," said the nine;
So they croaked and they splashed
    Where the quiet pools shine.

Over in the meadow,
    In a sly little den,
Lived a gray mother-spider
    And her little spiders ten.
"Spin," said the mother,
    "We spin," said the ten;
So they spun lace webs
    In their sly little den.

Monkeys

THE funniest thing in the world, I know,
Is watchin' the monkeys in the show!
Jumpin' and runnin' and racin' roun',
'Way up the top o' the pole, then down!
First they're here, an' then they're there,
An' just almost any an' everywhere!
Screechin' and scratchin' wherever they go,
They're the funniest thing in the world, I know!

—James Whitcomb Riley

From "The Funniest Thing in the World" in *Rhymes of Childhood*, by James Whitcomb Riley, copyright 1890, 1918, used by special permission of the publishers, The Bobbs-Merrill Company.

126

The Right Time to Laugh

AN AUSTRALIAN TALE

IN A DENSE Australian thicket, a lyrebird scratching in the ground once found a choice bit of food. So he spread his tail and rejoiced.

Just then along came a frog. "Good morning, friend," said the frog, as he sat down very solemnly and waited to be invited to share the feast. But the lyrebird took his food and flew up into a tree.

"My friend," said the frog, feeling slighted, "yesterday you dined with me. Don't you have a bite to spare for me today?"

"Certainly!" said the lyrebird, for he did not wish to appear as greedy as he was. "You may have a bite of my food. Just come right up and get it!"

"I can't come up," said the frog. "I've no wings with which to fly, and my feet were not made for climbing."

But the lyrebird, looking about, spied a vine trailing down from the tree with one end on the ground.

"Take hold of the vine," said he, "and I will pull you up." So the frog caught hold of the vine and the lyrebird pulled him up slowly until he was on a level with the branch where the lyrebird was sitting.

"I thank you, my friend," said the frog. He was about to hop down beside the food he desired, when the lyrebird let go of the vine and the frog dropped — kerplunk — to the ground. The lyrebird, thinking he had played a very fine joke on his friend, laughed and laughed and laughed, and he ate his dinner all by himself.

But the frog was very angry. He sat down below and sulked, thinking of nothing but the trick which the lyrebird had played on him.

"Well, I'll pay him back!" the frog told himself. "I'll pay him back, I will!"

So he hopped to the neighboring river, where the lyrebird got his water, and he drank and drank and drank. He drank till he swallowed not only all the water in that river, but all the water in all the rivers and all the lakes in Australia! Then he sat, quite puffed out with the water he had swallowed, and solemnly blinked his eyes.

Soon the lyrebird wanted a drink; but where was he to get it? There wasn't a river to turn to! The lyrebird got thirstier and thirstier until he was half-crazy for want of a drink of water. At last he was sufficiently punished for the wicked prank he had played to be very sorry for what he had done. And alas! he wasn't the only one who suffered; for not a beast or bird in all Australia could get a drink of water. One by one, they went to the frog and begged him to give out the waters. Dingo, the wild dog, went; Spiny, the anteater, went; Flying-fox, the great bat, went. And they said:

"Great frog, the lyrebird has done you wrong, but now he is very sorry and you are making us suffer who did you no wrong at all. Give forth the waters, we pray you."

But still the great frog sulked and would not answer a word. Then the lyrebird himself went before him and humbly begged his pardon. But the frog, stubborn as ever, unable to forget what the lyrebird had done to him, would not forgive the wrong. He sat as puffed up as before and solemnly blinked his eyes.

Then the great black swan went before him, and the white eagle, the emu, and all the other birds and beasts. But no matter how much they pleaded, the frog would not give back the water. So at length all the birds and the beasts got together and said:

"If the frog only knew how ridiculous he appears, sulking away like that, he would laugh at himself. Then the waters would gush from his mouth."

"Ah!" cried the anteater. "If that is the case, let us *make* him laugh and give up the rivers."

So they all stood in a circle around the solemn old frog and performed their funniest antics. They brought out the duck-billed platypus, and backed him up to the frog, who, looking at the creature's furry back, of course expected him to have the face of an animal. Then they turned the platypus around. There was the face of a bird with a flat, absurd bill like a duck's in the place where a snout ought to be. But the frog never smiled the slightest smile.

It seemed nothing would cause the frog to laugh, until at last they brought out an eel who stood on the tip of his long, long tail, and danced. He wiggled and twisted; he wriggled and swayed. The corners of the frog's mouth began to turn up. His lips began to twitch. His nose began to wrinkle, and all of a sudden he opened his mouth wide and he let out a mighty laugh. He laughed and he laughed and he laughed. As he laughed, the waters gushed from his mouth and filled up all the rivers and all the lakes in Australia.

"I was a silly old frog to sulk like that!" he cried.

Then the lyrebird and the wild dog and the anteater and the flying-fox and the opossum and the black swan, the white eagle and the emu, the duck-billed platypus and the kangaroo all hurried to get the drink which they so sorely needed.

The Ugly Duckling

RETOLD FROM HANS CHRISTIAN ANDERSEN

ONCE a mother duck sat on her eggs in the barnyard. At last the eggs began to crack and a lot of fluffy, yellow ducklings pecked their way out of the shells. But the mother duck looked and saw that one big egg had not hatched.

"How very strange!" said she. "That's a queer looking egg! It's not at all like the rest." But she sat on the egg a while longer, until, by and by, it cracked and out of it tumbled something, a clumsy little gray something, having a great long neck.

"My, what an ugly duckling!" said Mother Duck to herself. But she called "Quack, quack," to her brood and took them down to the water. In plumped the little ducklings. The water dashed over them, splash, but they all bobbed up again safely and floated along on the water as lightly as little toy ships.

"Well," said the Mother, "at least that ugly duckling can swim!" And after a time on the water, she called her whole brood to her. "We're going to the barnyard," she said. "I want to introduce you to the other ducks and the geese, the turkeys and the chickens. So mind your manners, children. Say 'Quack' just as I have taught you and keep your toes turned in!" Off she went with her ducklings trailing along behind her.

"A fine family, Madame Duck," clucked the chickens.

"Oh, but look at that one terribly ugly duckling!" quacked a pert little Mr. Duck. And he flew at the poor little creature and began to peck and bite him.

"Let him be!" said Mother Duck. "He is doing no harm."

"He's so queer, I have to whack him!" said pert little Mr. Duck. Then all the chickens and geese, the other ducks and the turkeys began to notice how ugly was that one strange, little duckling and they all began to peck and bite him, to push him around the yard, and make fun of his queer appearance. The Turkey Cock puffed himself up and went after him, "Gobble, gobble!" Even the little duck's own brothers and sisters pecked him. They bit him and shoved him around until he was at his wit's end. Then, one day, when all the barnyard was chasing and pestering him, he flew over the hedge and away.

THE UGLY DUCKLING

He half ran and half flew until he was all tired out. Then he settled down in a marsh. He did so need to rest. But here there were wild ducks to mock him.

"What sort of creature are you?" they cried. "You are certainly frightfully ugly!" And they flipped their tails in his face and left him alone to himself.

By and by, as he swam around, lonely, some wild geese came flying by. "I say, ugly creature," they called, "we've taken a fancy to you. Come, fly along with us!"

But, just at that moment, bang! Some hunters shot at the geese and they fell down, plump, in the water. Bang! bang! went the guns. Whole flocks of geese flew up out of the reeds and rushes, and dogs ran into the swamp, dashing and splashing around. The duckling was terribly frightened. He hid till the chase was over, then he ran away from the marsh.

Over the fields he ran until he came to a cottage. The door was open a crack, so he slipped into the house. There he saw a cat, a hen, and an old woman.

"What on earth is that?" asked the woman.

"A very strange creature," said the cat.

"Can you lay eggs?" asked the hen.

"No," said the poor little duckling.

"Can you purr?" asked the cat.

"No," said the poor little duckling.

"Then what use are you?" snapped the cat.

"No use," thought the poor duckling and he scurried out of the house and took refuge on a pond.

Slowly the summer passed. Leaves turned to gold and scarlet, then withered into brown and danced about in the wind. The sky grew gray and cold, and clouds hung heavy with snow. Then one evening just as the sunset shone red on a wintery world, a flock of great, beautiful birds appeared on the edge of the pond. They were a dazzling white with long, graceful, waving necks. Never had the ugly duckling seen anything so beautiful before.

THE UGLY DUCKLING

Uttering a strange, piercing cry, the birds spread their broad, white wings and flew off toward the warm southland. The duckling circled madly around on the little pond. He craned his neck after those birds. Then he, too, uttered a cry, a strange, piercing, longing cry. He did so want to go with them. They were such beautiful things.

All winter long he dreamed of those beautiful, great, white birds. The weather grew colder and colder and the duckling had to keep swimming, no matter how tired he was, to keep his one fishing hole from freezing into ice. At last all the pond froze over and the duckling was frozen in tight. Then a man came along and saw him. The man took his wooden shoe, hammered the ice from the duckling, and carried him home to his wife.

"What a nice little plaything!" cried the children of the house and they ran to pick him up. But the duckling was now so afraid of every creature he met that he thought the children would harm him. In a fright he rushed into the milk pan and the milk spurted up every which way all over the floor and the room. The woman let out a loud shriek. And the duckling, still more frightened, flew into the butter cask, then in and out of the meal tub. The woman ran for the tongs, intending to hit the wild creature, and the children fell over each other chasing the frightened duckling and

screaming with noisy laughter. Out the door flew the duckling and away into the night.

All winter long he looked after himself in a world of snow and ice. But, by and by, the sun began to shine warmly again, the larks began to sing, and spring came fresh and green, covering the earth with flowers. Then the ugly duckling, one day, found himself in a garden where the apple trees were in bloom and sweet-smelling purple lilacs hung over the shores of a lake. All at once he saw two beautiful, stately white birds, the very same kind of birds of which he had dreamed all winter. They slid into the lake, gliding gracefully over the water and arching their fine, white necks.

"Look! Look! The swans have come!" cried some children, rushing from a house. The duckling was very sad. The beauty of those fine swans made him feel ugly and lonely.

"I will fly to them," he said, "even though they peck me to pieces!" And he, too, slid into the lake and swam toward the beautiful swans. They turned and started toward him.

"Now they'll go at me," he thought, and he bowed his head to meet their attack; but, as he bent down his head, he

saw himself in the water. For the very first time that spring he saw his own reflection. And lo, he was no longer an ugly, dark-gray bird. He was white! He was stately! He had a long, graceful neck! He was splendid! He was beautiful! He, himself, was a swan! The other swans came up, not to peck, but to welcome him. Round and round him they swam; they stroked him with their bills; they bent their long necks before him. And the children threw bread crumbs to him and cried aloud in their joy, "There's a beautiful, new swan this year! He's the finest one on the lake."

All at once the swan's sadness melted into joy.

"How happy I am!" he thought. "I never even dreamed that I could be so happy when I was the ugly duckling. It doesn't matter in the least having been born in a duckyard if one comes out of a swan's egg!"

In *The Swan*, Camille Saint-Saëns shows us in music this beautiful, white bird gliding calmly over smooth waters, broken only by little ripples. Majestically lifting its head, the swan circles about before us, then swims off out of sight.

The Clucking Hen

WILL you take a walk with me,
    My little wife, today?
There's barley in the barley field,
    And hayseed in the hay."

"Thank you," said the clucking hen;
    "I've something else to do;
I'm busy sitting on my eggs,
    I cannot walk with you."

The clucking hen sat on her nest,
    She made it on the hay;
And warm and snug beneath her breast
    A dozen white eggs lay.

Crack, crack, went all the eggs,
    Out dropped the chickens small;
"Cluck," said the clucking hen,
    "Now I have you all.

"Come along, my little chicks,
    I'll take a walk with you."
"Hello!" said the barn-door cock.
    "Cock-a-doodle-do!"
          —From *Aunt Effie's Rhymes*

SCHOOL is over,
Oh, what fun!
Lessons finished,
Play begun.
Who'll run fastest,
You or I?
Who'll laugh loudest?
Let us try.
—*Kate Greenaway**

*Kate Greenaway is famous for her charming little pictures of children. As she began to draw the quaint costumes, inspired by her love of English country people, she dressed dolls as models in order to experiment with color and style

A German Evening

FROM the woods, the father, coming,
  Gladly now is turning homeward
To his dear and cheerful cottage.
Homeward all the sheep come bleating,
And the herds of cattle lowing,
Homeward to their stalls are going.
Streets and markets grow more quiet;
Round the bright and kindly lamplight
All the family comes together,
And the town-gate closes creaking.

—*Wilhelm Schiller*

A Bohemian Evening

NIGHT has called the sun to rest
  Homeward wind the flocks of sheep.
Day for children, too, is over,
Come, my children, come to sleep.

—*Czechoslovakian Nursery Rhyme*

A Belgian Morning

OH, the merry tinkling sounds
    Every morning
Of the milk-carts on their rounds,
And the yelping of the dogs;
And on the golden straw
As they jolt the road along,
The big fat cans of copper bright
Beneath the summer sun.

—Emile Cammaerts

A Swedish Evening

DID you ever hear the cowbells, did you ever hear the
    singing,
Floating down the meadow when the evening shadows fall?
Cows are all a-lowing; down the path they're swinging,
Hurrying in answer to the milkmaid's call.
Over field and pasture hear the calling come—
Come, Lily! Come, Lily! Come, Lily! Come!

—Gustaf Fröding

The Bird's Convention

ALL the birds have come together!
  All the birds that I could mention,
Meet to hold a big convention!

How they cluster, how they muster,
How they flitter, flutter, fluster!
Now they dart with gleaming feather.
Now they cuddle all together!

—Aristophanes

Answer to a Child's Question

DO you ask what the birds say? The sparrow, the dove?
  The linnet and thrush say, "I love and I love!"
In the winter they're silent—the wind is so strong.
What it says I don't know, but it sings a loud song.
But green leaves and blossoms and sunny warm weather,
And singing and loving—all come back together.
But the lark is so brimful of gladness and love,
The green fields below him, the blue sky above,
That he sings and he sings and forever sings he:
"I love my Love and my Love loves me!"

—Samuel Taylor Coleridge

How the Finch Got Her Colors

A FLEMISH LEGEND

ONCE upon a time all the birds were gray; they had no colors at all. Then the Great Bird, who ruled over them, called them all together. He showed them the rainbow up in the sky shimmering with red, yellow, green, blue, and violet. And he told them that he meant to give each of them one of those splendid colors. At once they began pushing and shoving and crowding about him.

"Let me have first choice! I'll take green," screeched the parrot.

"Give me blue! I want blue!" piped the bluebird.

"I'll take yellow," cried the canary.

But, during all this clamor, one little bird sat quietly and waited her turn to speak. That was the Finch.

"Now you each have a splendid color," said the Great Bird, "and it's well that you have for every single color is gone."

But, just at that moment, the Great Bird spied the little Finch. "Come here, little Finch!" he cried. "Why have you asked for nothing?"

"I was waiting my turn," said the Finch.

"But now all the colors are gone," said the Great Bird.

The earliest examples of musical tone were imitations of the voices of nature, and many compositions for the flute or the voice imitate the song of the bird. "Ye Birds without Number" from the opera, I Pagliacci, by Leoncavallo expresses the voices of birds.

143

"Dear, dear, dearie," sighed the Finch, "must I then always be gray?"

Suddenly the Great Bird, called all the other birds back just as they were about to fly away in their splendid colors.

"Be always gray," he cried, "because you would not push and shove! Because you would not screech what you wanted ahead of all the rest! No, indeed, you shall not!"

Then he made all the other birds pass in order before him. From each he took a bit of color. From the cardinal a bit of red, from the blue bird a bit of blue, from the parrot a bit of green, from the canary a bit of yellow, from the grackle a bit of purple. And he gave all these bits of color to the little Finch. Then lo and behold, the little Finch shone with all the tints of the rainbow. Not one color alone was hers, but all—all melting beautifully into each other. Thus it came about that the prettiest bird of the air was the little wee Finch who waited her turn.

The Sheep and the Pig That Made a Home

A NORSE FOLK TALE

ONCE upon a time there was a Sheep, and he started out into the world to build himself a home. First he went to the Pig and he said:

"There is nothing like having a home of your own. If you are of my way of thinking, we will go into the woods and build a house and live by ourselves."

Yes, the Pig was quite willing. "It's nice to be in good company," said he, and off they started.

When they had got a bit on the way, they met a Goose.

"Good day, my good people. Where are you off to?" said the Goose.

"Good day," answered the Sheep. "We're off to the woods to build a house and live by ourselves."

"Why shouldn't I join you?" said the Goose.

"No house can be built by gobbling and quacking," said the Pig. "What can you do to help build?"

"I can pluck moss and stuff it into the holes between the logs so the house will be warm and cozy," said the Goose.

"Very well, you may come along then," said the Sheep and the Pig. When they had gone a bit farther, they met a Hare.

"Good day, my good people," said the Hare. "Where are you going to-day?"

"Good day," answered the Sheep. "We're off to the woods to build a house and live by ourselves."

"I've a good mind to go with you," said the Hare.

"But what can you do to help us build?" asked the Pig. "Nothing at all, I should say."

"There is always something for willing hands to do in this world," said the Hare. "I have sharp teeth to gnaw pegs with, and I have paws to knock them into the walls; so I'll do very well for a carpenter."

"Well, you may come along with us then," said the Sheep, the Pig, and the Goose.

When they had gone a bit farther, they met a Cock.

"Good day, my good people," said the Cock. "Where are you all going to-day?"

"Good day," said the Sheep. "We're off to the woods to build a house and live by ourselves."

"Well, it's better to have your own roost than to sit on a neighbor's roost and crow," said the Cock. "I should like to go to the woods and build a house with you."

"Flapping and crowing is fine for noise, but it won't build a house," said the Pig. "How can you help us build?"

"It is not well to live in a house where there is neither a dog nor a cock to awaken you in the morning," said the Cock. "I rise very early and can awaken you all with my crowing."

"Early to rise makes one happy and wealthy and wise," said the Pig, who found it very hard to wake up in the morning. "Let the Cock come along then."

So they all set off to the woods and built the house. The Pig cut down the trees and the Sheep dragged them home; the Hare was the carpenter, and gnawed pegs and hammered them into walls and roof; the Goose plucked moss and stuffed it into the little holes between the logs; the Cock crew and took care that they did not oversleep themselves in the mornings. And when the house was finished, they all lived happily together. And they often said:

"It's pleasant to travel both
East and West
But home is, after all,
the best."

148

Building the Bridge

ADAPTED FROM A RUSSIAN FOLK SONG

IN the forest, in the forest stood a big pine tree. Green and shaggy in the forest stood a big pine tree.

Men came there with axes— Bang, bang, bang with axes they cut the pine tree down.

They took a saw and sawed it—Zim, zim, zip, they sawed it. They sawed it into planks.

They took the planks and laid them. They laid them one by one across a shining river.

They nailed the planks with hammers—Rap, tap, tap, with hammers they nailed the boards down fast.

And so they made a bridge. They made a great big bridge across the shining river. And who will go across that bridge? Michael, Michael, he will go, go across the bridge!

M.S.
HURFORD

The Little Dog Waltz

ONCE a lady had a little dog. He was a lively little dog and he loved to tear around madly after rats and cats, or just after nothing at all. Well, one day a man came to see the lady. His name was Mr. Chopin and as he sat talking with the lady, the little dog lay beside them.

All at once, with a bound the little dog sprang up. He just had to have a chase. He couldn't sit still any longer and he had to chase after something, so he thought he'd chase after his tail. Round and round he tore, round and round and round, but the faster and faster he ran, the faster his tail ran, too. He just couldn't catch that tail. He ran and he ran and he ran until he began to get dizzy. Then he tumbled down in a heap. For a time he just rested. Then he caught sight of that crazy tail of his again. There it was wagging behind him, inviting another chase. In a moment he was on his feet whirling as madly as before.

As he ran round and round in circles, his mistress began to laugh. "If I could play the piano as you can," she said to Mr. Chopin, "I'd make up a waltz so the little fellow could have music for that whirligig he's dancing!"

*The lady whose little dog inspired this waltz was the great French writer who went by the name of George Sand. And the man who composed *The Little Dog Waltz* or *The Minute Waltz*, as it is also called, was the half French, half Polish musician, Frederic Chopin (1809-1849) known also for his gay *Mazurka* and other Polish dances.

Then Mr. Chopin laughed, too. He went to the piano, sat down on the stool and, in no more than one minute, he played that whole playful chase right on the piano keys. Round and round went his music, whirling and circling and whirling, just like the little dog. He even put in the part where the little dog got dizzy and tumbled down in a heap. For an instant the music rested, then it started to chase again for all the world like the dog.

And the lady said, "Mr. Chopin, I think you should call your waltz *The Minute Waltz* because you can play it in a minute."

But Mr. Chopin said, "It was the little dog who made this waltz. I shall call it *The Little Dog Waltz*."

Nurse's Song

WILLIAM BLAKE *

WHEN the voices of children are heard on the green,
 And laughing is heard on the hill,
My heart is at rest within my breast,
 And everything else is still.

"Then come home, my children, the sun is gone down,
 And the dews of the night arise;
Come, come, leave off play, and let us away
 Till the morning appears in the skies."

"No, no, let us play, for it is yet day,
 And we cannot go to sleep;
Besides in the sky the little birds fly,
 And the hills are all covered with sheep."

"Well, well, go and play till the light fades away,
 And then go home to bed."
The little ones leaped, and shouted, and laughed,
 And all the hills echoéd.

*Early writers for children all thought they must preach; but the poet, William Blake, in a flash of pure genius wrote *Songs of Innocence* in 1789, full of the joyous spirit of childhood and with no thought of preaching.

Late

JOSEPHINE PRESTON PEABODY

MY Father brought somebody up,
    To show us all, asleep.
They came as softly up the stairs
    As you could creep.

They whispered in the doorway there,
    And looked at us awhile.
I had my eyes shut up; but I
    Could feel him smile.

I shut my eyes up close, and lay
    As still as I could keep;
Because I knew he wanted us
    To be asleep.

Nonsense Rhymes

EDWARD LEAR

"PLEASE give me a ride on your back,"
    Said the duck to the kangaroo:
"I would sit quite still and say nothing
        but 'Quack'!
    The whole of the long day through;
And we'd go to the Dee, and the
        Jelly Bo Lee,
Over the land and over the sea:
    Please take me a ride!   Oh, do!"
    Said the duck to the kangaroo.

THERE was an old man
    with a beard,
Who said, "It is just
    as I feared!
Two owls and a hen,
    four larks and a wren,
Have all built their nests
    in my beard!"

The Bee, the Mouse and the Bum-Clock

AN IRISH TALE

ONCE there lived a poor woman who had only one son, Jack. They hadn't a thing in the world but a black cow, a red cow, and a spotted cow. One day the mother said, "Jack, we have nothing at all to eat except a few potatoes. Go to the fair tomorrow and sell the big black cow."

So Jack set out at sun-up, driving the cow before him. But, when he came to the fair, he saw a big crowd of people, all of them looking at something. Pushing his way through the crowd, Jack saw a queer little man with a bee who could play a wee harp, a mouse, and a little brown beetle which went by the name of a bum-clock. The queer little man gave a whistle; the bee began to play the harp, the mouse and the

bum-clock stood up, took hold of each other's shoulders, and started in to dance. And all the men, women, and children; horses, cows, and chickens; ducks and geese began to dance. The pots and pans, the wheels and reels started in to jig. Jack's cow stood on her hind legs; Jack took hold of her hoofs and they danced all over the town.

But, when the man picked up the creatures and put them in his pocket, the people, the beasts, the pots, the pans, the wheels, and the reels all stopped dancing at once.

"Jack," said the man, "why don't you buy my dancers?"

"I should like to," said Jack, "but I haven't any money."

"You have a fine cow," said the man. "I will give you the bee and the harp in exchange for your cow."

"But my mother is sad and in need. We are very poor at home," said Jack. "I must sell the cow for money."

"Oh," said the man, "if your mother is sad, take her this bee and the harp. She'll laugh until she is merry."

"Maybe you're right," said Jack. So he gave the man the cow, took the bee and the harp, and put them in his pocket.

When he got home, his mother ran out the door to greet him. "I see you sold the cow," she said, looking very glad.

"Yes, I did very well!" Jack took the bee and the harp from his pocket and set them on the ground. Then he whistled to the bee and the bee began to play the harp. The mother let out a big laugh and she and Jack started to dance, the pots and pans, the wheels and reels all began to jig and the very house itself went hopping around on the ground. But when Jack picked up the bee and the harp, everything stood still. The mother laughed a while longer but, when she stopped, she cried angrily:

"Silly boy, to bring home no money for the cow. Our potatoes are nearly gone and we shall have nothing to eat. Go tomorrow to the fair again and sell the big red cow."

So Jack was off with sun-up, driving the big red cow. But when he got to the fair, there was the crowd of people and there was the queer little man with the mouse and the bum-clock. The man gave a whistle as before and the mouse and the bum-clock danced. And all the people and animals, the pots and pans, the wheels and reels started in to jig. The very houses danced and hopped around on the ground. But, when the man picked up the creatures, everything stopped dancing.

"Jack," said the man. "I'll trade my mouse for your cow."

"My mother is still sad. I must sell my cow," said Jack.

"But," said the man, "if your mother is sad, this mouse is what she needs. When she sees it dance while the bee plays the harp, she will laugh fit to split her sides."

"Maybe you're right," said Jack. And he gave the man the cow, took the mouse, and put it in his pocket.

When he got home, his mother ran out the door to meet him.

"Surely this time, Jack, you have brought home money," she said.

158

BEE, MOUSE AND BUM CLOCK

"No," said Jack. "I've no money, but see what I got for the cow." And he took out of his pocket the mouse, the bee, and the harp. Then he whistled to them; the bee began to play the harp and the mouse stood up on its hind legs and started in to dance. The mother let out a big laugh and she and Jack started to dance. The pots and pans, the wheels and reels all began to jig and the very house itself went hopping around on the ground. But when Jack picked up the creatures, everything stood still. The mother laughed awhile longer, but when she stopped, she was angry.

"You silly boy," she said, "our potatoes are all gone now. Go tomorrow to the fair again and sell the spotted cow."

So Jack was off with sun-up, driving the spotted cow. But when he got to the fair, there was the big crowd of people, and there was the queer little man, whistling to the bum-clock. The bum-clock started to dance and all the people and animals, the pots and pans, the wheels and reels began to jig. The very houses danced, hopping around on the ground.

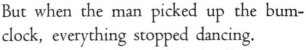

But when the man picked up the bum-clock, everything stopped dancing.

"Hello, Jack," said the man. "You must surely buy this bum-clock to make your dancers complete. I'll trade it for your cow."

"But my mother is sadder than ever. I must sell my cow," said Jack.

"Ah," said the man, "but think, when your mother sees this bum-clock dancing with the mouse while the bee plays on the harp, she will laugh all her sadness away!"

"Maybe you're right," said Jack. And he gave the man the cow, took the bum-clock from him and put it in his pocket.

When he reached home again, his mother ran out to meet him. "Surely you've brought money this time," she said. But Jack took the bum-clock, the mouse, the bee, and the harp from his pocket. He set them on the floor and whistled. The bee began to play the harp, the mouse and the bum-clock stood up and started to dance together. Jack's mother laughed a big laugh and she and Jack started to dance. The pots and pans, the wheels and reels all began to jig and the very house itself went hopping around on the ground. But when Jack picked up the creatures, everything stood still. The mother laughed a while longer, but when she stopped laughing, she cried as if her heart would break.

BEE, MOUSE AND BUM CLOCK

"You silly boy," she said, "we haven't a thing to eat now and all our cows are gone. There's nothing left to sell."

Well now Jack did feel foolish. Yes, he had been a simpleton. All the cows gone and no money! He went out to take a walk and scold himself on the way. But suddenly on the road he met a little old woman.

"Jack," said the little old woman, "why don't you go to the castle of the King of Ireland? He has a beautiful daughter who has not laughed in seven years. Hark now, he has promised to give both the girl and his kingdom to any man who will make the sad little princess laugh three times."

"I'm off this moment," said Jack and he ran back to his mother, kissed her merrily, and started off for the castle.

Now the king and his sad little daughter were sitting with all the court people on gold and silver chairs out in front of the castle. All at once there came Jack with the little bee and his harp, the little mouse and the bum-clock, all tied together by a string, hopping and skipping behind him. And when the king and his people saw that sight, they started in to laugh The princess opened her mouth and laughed fit to split her sides.

"Ah, my lady," said Jack, "that's once I've made you laugh!" Then Jack drew the creatures up in a little circle and whistled. The bee began to play the harp, the mouse and the bum-clock stood up and started in to dance. And the king and all his people, the pots and pans, the wheels and reels, the very castle itself all hopped and jigged and jumped. The princess opened her mouth and laughed fit to split her sides.

"Ah, my lady," said Jack, "that's twice I've made you laugh." But what was Jack to do next to make her laugh a third time. She now looked as solemn as an owl. The little mouse came to his aid. She swished her little tail and swept it in the bum-clock's mouth, and the bum-clock started to cough and bounce around like a ball. Then the princess opened her mouth and laughed fit to split her sides.

"Ah, my lady," said Jack, "that's thrice I've made you laugh!" Then the king was very glad and he gave Jack the princess and his kingdom. And Jack sent for his mother and she lived in the castle and they never were poor any more.

162

The Song of the Bee[*]

BUZZ-ZZ, Buzz-zz, Buzz-zz!
  This is the song of the bee.
His legs are all yellow,
  This jolly good fellow,
A very hard worker is he!

—Old Jingle

The Purple Cow[**]

I NEVER Saw a Purple Cow;
  I never Hope to See one;
But I can Tell you, Anyhow,
I'd rather See than Be one.

—Gelett Burgess

[*]*The Bee* by François Schubert delightfully depicts in music the bee buzzing, darting from flower to flower, and disappearing in a blossom. [**]From *The Burgess Nonsense Book.* By arrangement with the publishers, Frederick A. Stokes Company.

163

Little Hansworst

HANSWORST is a funny little fellow. Come, I shall tell you his story. Once in old days in Holland, a merry little bird laid a merry little egg in a merry little nest in a merry little bush. By and by there came a tipping, a tapping and a pecking from inside the merry little egg. All at once the shell went crack! And out of the egg crawled what? Out crawled little Hansworst. No sooner did he see the light, than he cut a crazy caper, stood on his head and said, "I will be merry as long as I live." Then he painted on his breast a very large red heart.

"People shall know," said he, "that I am a brave boy, and my heart is in the right place!" Down the dike ran Hans and over the green meadows! Sometimes he stood on his head; sometimes he turned handsprings or bounced like a rubber ball. Out dashed a little rabbit. A brave boy was Hansworst. Well anyhow, he said he was! But still, when he saw that rabbit, Hans turned and ran away.

164

So very fast did Hans run that his
legs scarcely touched the ground, the
tails of his yellow jacket floated out
in the wind like a pair of yellow wings,
and he seemed to fly over the earth.

Just then along came a man, and what should he see but
this yellow thing flying over the meadows? "Ha," said the
man to himself, "that's a nice kind of birdie!" And he
reached out his great long arm, caught Hans by the seat
of his breeches, and put him
in his pocket. Then he took
him on along home. A pretty
little cottage it was to which
the man took Hansworst,
a neat, little, red-brick cottage with pretty green-and-
white shutters. Hans peeped
from the man's pocket and
saw it as they drew near.

He didn't mind being taken into such a place as that! No, not at all! Why should he? He thought it would be great fun to climb on the shining brass teakettle over the charcoal teastove, and make out all the pictures that were painted on the blue-and-white plates in the rack on the wall above. But alack! If Master Hansworst thought the man-of-the-house was going to set him free to play such pranks as that, he was very much mistaken. The man took Hansworst to the window, and there above the geraniums hung a nice, little, wicker bird-cage. The man put Hansworst inside; then bang, he closed the door!

Well, how was that for Hansworst! The birds crowded round the newcomer, cheeping and chirping and fluttering. But, in no time at all, Hansworst was whistling and singing and he and the birds were fast friends.

LITTLE HANSWORST

This was all very well, and Hans proved to be as merry inside the cage as out, but still, there was certainly one thing he did not like at all. He simply could not eat birdseed. It had no taste whatever. And, when the bird-seed box was newly filled in the cage and  the birds ate the seeds with delight, Hansworst was very miserable. One day the woman of the house laid the table for dinner, in the window below the cage. Then the man sat down at the table and the woman brought him a sausage, a nice fat sausage on a plate. Um, but that sausage smelled good! And Hans was very hungry! Now it chanced that, just as the man was about to eat the sausage, the grandfather's clock in the corner struck the hour of twelve; and the man paused—with fork in air—to watch the man-in-the-moon, that was painted on the clock's face, rise from behind a church steeple and go rolling across the sky to sink behind a townhall.

There lay the fat little sausage, unnoticed, on the plate, smiling, as it were, at Hans, and smelling, oh so good! Hans reached his little hand down through the wire of the cage and seized it. Oh, but it was good! He ate every single crumb.

When the man-of-the-house looked around, he found that his sausage had vanished. Good 'lack, but he was astonished!

Well, the same thing happened the next day and the next day and the next. Always his sausage vanished just as the dock struck twelve. Finally, on the fifth day, the man fell to wondering so much about what had happened to his sausages, that he left off watching the clock as soon as it struck two strokes, and he turned around just in time to see little Hans-worst eating the last crumbs of his sausage.

LITTLE HANSWORST

"Whoever heard the like! A bird eating sausage!" he cried. And he fell to scratching his head till a bright idea struck him. "If this bird eats meat, he can't be a bird!" he cried and he stood up and looked in the cage. Sure enough, he saw that Hansworst was not a bird at all, never had been, and never would be! So he wasted not a moment, but opened the door of the cage and shouted, "Out you go!"

Hansworst took such a leap as he had never taken in all his life before. Out of the window he leapt, zipping along through the air, and he never came down to earth till he sailed in the window of a toyshop some distance up the street!

What a place that Hansworst was in now! Tin soldiers all about, and dolls and hobby horses, and all the animals of Noah's Ark! That was what Hansworst liked! That was a merry crowd! He rode the hobby horses, he danced with the dolls, he marched with the soldiers, he ordered the animals in and out of Noah's Ark, he climbed the wooden trees. There was no end to his fun.

But the next day there came to the toyshop a man with a little doll's theatre. It was this man's business to go from fair to fair, when the country people came into town, and to set up his little theatre in the market square, where he made all his wooden dolls play antics for the crowd.

"But," said the man, looking sad, "my two chief actors are very bad dolls—Mr. and Mrs. John Klaasen. Day in and day out they quarrel and hit each other. It's enough to bring tears to the eyes. They're all banged up already. To bring me a little joy, I must buy some merry fellow. Pray you show me the merriest fellow you have in all your shop."

Now, of course, the toy-seller knew Hansworst was the merriest fellow to be found in all the world. So he took Hans off a toy elephant on which he had been riding and sold him to the man. Then the man took Hansworst away from all his fun in the toyshop. Perhaps you'd think this was enough to make even Hansworst sad. John Klaasen and his wife were a sorry pair to travel with, always hitting and banging each other till they broke their wooden heads.

LITTLE HANSWORST

But the very first time Hansworst bounced out on the stage of that theatre and saw all the good folk waiting for him to make them laugh, he quite forgot everything else. He knew that at last he had found his right place in the world. He skipped, he hopped, he cracked jokes till the people held their sides for laughter.

"Hansworst! Hansworst!" they shouted. And the next time these good folk heard that Hansworst had come to town, they crowded from all ways to see him.

So it was that Hansworst became the most famous clown in Holland. Year in and year out, he played with John Klaasen and his wife in the little puppet show, and to this very day one has but to say, "Hansworst," and the faces of all jolly Dutchmen will blossom like magic with smiles.

How the Brazilian Beetles Got Their Gorgeous Coats*

Elsie Spicer Eells

IN Brazil the beetles have beautiful, coloured, hard-shelled coats upon their backs like precious stones. Once upon a time, years and years ago, they had ordinary plain, brown coats. This is how it happened that the Brazilian beetle earned a new coat.

One day a little brown beetle was crawling along a wall when a big grey rat ran out of a hole in the wall and looked down scornfully at the little beetle. "Oh, ho!" he said to the beetle, "how slowly you crawl along. You'll never get anywhere in the world. Just look at me and see how fast I can run."

The big grey rat ran to the end of the wall, wheeled around, and came back to the place where the little beetle was slowly crawling along at only a tiny distance from where the rat had left her.

"Don't you wish that you could run like that?" said the big grey rat to the little brown beetle.

"You are surely a fast runner," replied the little brown beetle, politely. Her mother had taught her that a really polite

*Taken from *Fairy Tales from Brazil*. Copyright, 1917, by Dodd, Mead & Company, Inc.

beetle never boasts about her own accomplishments.

A bright green-and-gold parrot in the mango tree over the wall had heard the conversation. "How would you like to race with the beetle?" he asked the big grey rat. "I live next door to the tailor bird," he added, "and just to make the race exciting, I'll offer a bright-coloured coat as a prize to the one who wins the race. You may choose for it any colour you like and I'll have it made to order."

"I'd like a yellow coat with stripes like the tiger's," said the big grey rat, looking over his shoulder at his gaunt grey sides, as if he were already admiring his new coat.

"I'd like a beautiful, bright-coloured, new coat, too," said the little brown beetle.

The big grey rat laughed long and loud until his gaunt grey sides were shaking. "Why, you talk just as if you thought you had a chance to win the race," he said, when he could speak.

The bright green-and-gold parrot set the royal palm tree at the top of the cliff as the goal of the race. He gave the signal to start and then he flew away to

the royal palm tree to watch for the end of the race. The big grey rat ran as fast as he could. Then he thought how very tired he was getting. "What's the use of hurrying?" he said to himself. "The little brown beetle cannot possibly win."

Then he started to run more slowly, but every time his heart beat, it said, "Hurry up! Hurry up!" The big grey rat decided that it was best to obey the little voice in his heart, so he hurried just as fast as he could.

When he reached the royal palm tree at the top of the cliff, he could hardly believe his eyes. There was the little brown beetle sitting quietly beside the bright green-and-gold parrot. The big grey rat had never been so surprised in all his life. "How did you ever manage to run fast enough to get here so soon?" he asked the little brown beetle as soon as he could catch his breath. "I flew here," said the little beetle.

"I did not know you could fly," said the big grey rat in a subdued little voice.

"After this," said the parrot, "never judge anyone by his looks alone. You never can tell where you may find concealed wings. You have lost the prize and the beetle has won it."

Then the parrot said to the little brown beetle, "What colour do you want your new coat to be?"

The little brown beetle looked up at the bright green-and-gold parrot, at the green-and-gold palm trees above their heads, at the golden sunshine upon the distant green hills. "I choose a coat of green-and-gold," she said. And from that day to this, the Brazilian beetle has worn a coat of green, with golden lights upon it.

THE BOASTER
ADAPTED FROM AESOP

A BOASTER boasted boastfully
He could do this and that;
His friends then said: "Sir Boaster,
Pray stop your silly chat!

"If you can do these marvels all,
No need to talk, my man;
Just *do* for us these wondrous things
That now you *say* you can!"

Precocious Piggy

W HERE are you going to, you little pig?"
"I'm leaving my mother, I'm growing so big!"
"So big, young pig,
So young, so big!
What! Leaving your mother, you foolish young pig!"

"Where are you going to, you little pig?"
"I've got a new spade, and I'm going to dig."
"To dig, little pig?
A little pig dig!
Well, I never saw a pig with a spade that could dig!"

"Where are you going to, you little pig?"
"Why, I'm going to have a nice ride in a gig!"
"In a gig, little pig?
What! A pig in a gig!
Well, I never saw a pig ride in a gig!"

"Where are you going to, you little pig?"
"Well, I'm going to the ball to dance a fine jig!"
"A jig, little pig?
A pig dance a jig!
Well, I never before saw a pig dance a jig!"

"Where are you going to, you little pig?"
"I'm going to the fair to run a fine rig."
"A rig, little pig?
A pig run a rig!
Well, I never before saw a pig run a rig!"

"Where are you going to, you little pig?"
"I'm going to the barber's to buy me a wig!"
"A wig, little pig?
A pig in a wig!
Why, whoever before saw a pig in a wig!"
—Thomas Hood (1799-1845)

The Turtle Who Could Not Stop Talking

AN EAST INDIAN FABLE

ONCE a Turtle lived in a muddy little pond, and he loved to crawl out in the sun and talk to everyone who passed. He talked to the beasts, he talked to the birds, and he talked to the fishes. In fact, he never stopped talking. Well, one day there came flying by two beautiful wild geese.

"Friend Turtle," cried the Geese, "Would you like to fly with us to our beautiful home far away? We live on a shining blue pool that is just as clear as glass."

The Turtle's own pool was muddy. A shining blue pool clear as glass—he would certainly like to see that!

"But how can I go with you? I have no wings," he said.

"Oh, we will take you," said the Geese, "if you promise to keep your mouth closed, and speak not a single word."

"Why of course I'll keep my mouth closed. I'll do just as you say," said the Turtle.

So the next day the Geese came back carrying with their feet a stick which they held between them.

"Take hold of this stick with your mouth," they said to the Turtle. "But don't say a word as we fly; for, if you do, you will lose your hold and fall down kerplunk to the ground."

"I'll do just as you say," said the Turtle, eager to depart.

So the Turtle took hold of the stick, and the Geese soared up in the air, carrying him between them. Over the treetops they flew and up in the bright blue sky. But as they passed over a village, the children down below saw their old friend, the Turtle.

"Oh, look at the Turtle!" they cried.

"I'm taking a long, long journey," the Turtle wanted to boast, but he remembered just in time and did not open his mouth.

"How silly he looks!" cried the children.

"Silly yourself!" the Turtle wanted to answer crossly; but he remembered just in time and did not open his mouth.

"How does he ever keep his mouth closed?" the children jeered. "Do you suppose he can really stop talking?"

This was too much for the Turtle.

"Of course I can stop talking!" he cried, and, as he opened his mouth to speak, he lost his hold on the stick and fell down, crash, at their feet.

"Poor little Turtle," said the children. "He really could not stop talking."

The Owl and the Pussy-Cat

EDWARD LEAR

THE Owl and the Pussy-Cat went to sea
In a beautiful pea-green boat:
They took some honey, and plenty of money
Wrapped up in a five-pound note.
The Owl looked up to the stars above,
And sang to a small guitar:
"O lovely Pussy, O Pussy, my love,
What a beautiful Pussy you are!"

Pussy said to the Owl, "You elegant fowl,
How charmingly sweet you sing!
Oh! let us be married! too long we have tarried;
But what shall we do for a ring?"
They sailed away, for a year and a day,
To the land where the bong-tree grows:
And there in a wood a Piggy-wig stood,
With a ring in the end of his nose.

"Dear Pig, are you willing to sell for one shilling
Your ring?" Said the Piggy, "I will."
So they took it away, and were married next day
By the Turkey who lives on the hill.
They dined on mince and slices of quince,
Which they ate with a runcible spoon;
And hand in hand, on the edge of the sand,
They danced by the light of the moon.

The Strange Adventure of
Baron Münchausen

ONCE there lived a very queer man by the name of Baron Münchausen. He was riding one day in Russia where all the world was covered with snow. By-and-by the sun went down. It began to get dark and the stars came out in the sky. So the Baron looked around to see if he could find some house where he could sleep that night and get a bite to eat. But he couldn't see a house or any living thing. All he could see was snow, snow, snow. So he said, "I'll have to sleep on the snow." And he jumped off his horse. But his horse was a frisky horse and the Baron was afraid he might run away if he wasn't tied up. So the Baron looked around again, trying to find something to which he might tie his horse. But there was only snow everywhere. Not a single thing could he see that stuck up above that snow. Then at last he spied what looked like the pointed stump of a little tree.

Baron Münchausen's Narrative of His Marvelous Travels and Campaigns in Russia, by the German writer Raspe (1785), is famous in literary history for its amusingly impossible adventures; and, even to this day, anyone telling an exaggerated story is called a Baron Münchausen.

So he tied the horse to the tree stump and lay down to sleep on the snow.

All night long the Baron slept. It was daylight when he woke up. But no sooner had he opened his eyes than he sat up in a hurry. For what was this he saw? He wasn't lying on the pile of snow on which he had gone to sleep. He was lying in the middle of a village! All around him were houses, houses! And there was a church towering up above him!

"This can't be! It just can't be!" the Baron cried. "There were no houses here last night!"

But after a time he saw it was true that he was in a village. And he started to think about his horse.

"Where in the world can my horse be?" he wondered. But he couldn't see a sign of the horse nor a sign of the tree stump to which he had tied him. Then all of a sudden —"Neigh! Neigh, neigh, neigh!" He heard his horse neighing somewhere up in the air above him. Looking up, up, up, above the tall church to the cross on top of it, he saw his horse hanging way up there, still tied fast by his bridle and dangling in the air. That was a surprise, I can tell you! But the truth was that the weather had grown much warmer. The snow had melted during the night, letting the Baron down on the ground. It had melted away from the church and the houses it had covered the night before. And when the Baron had tied his horse to what he thought was a tree stump sticking out of the snow, he had really tied him to the cross on top of the church. So there the poor horse now hung.

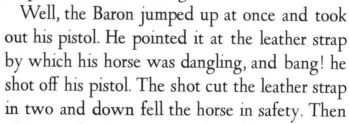

Well, the Baron jumped up at once and took out his pistol. He pointed it at the leather strap by which his horse was dangling, and bang! he shot off his pistol. The shot cut the leather strap in two and down fell the horse in safety. Then the Baron mounted his horse and went on his way again!

Old Shellover

COME!" said Old Shellover.
  "What?" says Creep.
"The horny old Gardener's fast
    asleep;
The fat cock Thrush
To his nest has gone,
And the dew shines bright
In the rising Moon;
Old Sallie Worm from her hole doth
    peep;
Come!" said Old Shellover.
"Ay!" said Creep.*

        —Walter De La Mare

The Song of the Flea

ONCE a King, be it noted
  had a fine and lusty flea,
And on this flea he doted,
  he cherished him tenderly;
So he sent off for his tailor
  and to the tailor spake,
'Please to measure this youngster
  and coat and breeches make!"
In velvet and in satin
He now was duly dressed,
He had rare jewels in his hat
And medals decked his breast!

    —from the Opera on Faust by Hector Berlioz

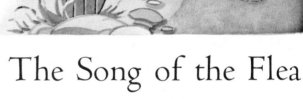

*From *Peacock Pie*. Used by courteous permission of Henry Holt & Company.

Jack Frost

GABRIEL SETOUN

THE door was shut, as doors should be,
Before you went to bed last night;
Yet Jack Frost has got in, you see,
And left your window silver white.

He must have waited till you slept;
And not a single word he spoke,
But penciled o'er the panes and crept
Away again before you woke.

And now you cannot see the trees
Nor fields that stretch beyond the lane;
But there are fairer things than these
His fingers traced on every pane.

From Child's World; used by the courteous permission of John Lane Company.

186

Rocks and castles towering high;
Hills and dales and streams and fields;
And knights in armour riding by,
With nodding plumes and shining shields.

And here are little boats, and there
Big ships with sails spread to the breeze;
And yonder, palm-trees waving fair
On islands set in silver seas.

And butterflies with gauzy wings;
And herds of cows and flocks of sheep;
And fruit and flowers and all the things
You see when you are sound asleep.

For, creeping softly underneath
The door when all the lights are out,
Jack Frost takes every breath you breathe
And knows the things you think about.

He paints them on the window-pane
In fairy lines with frozen steam;
And when you wake, you see again
The lovely things you saw in dream.

Dame Wiggins of Lee*

MARY E. SHARPE AND JOHN RUSKIN

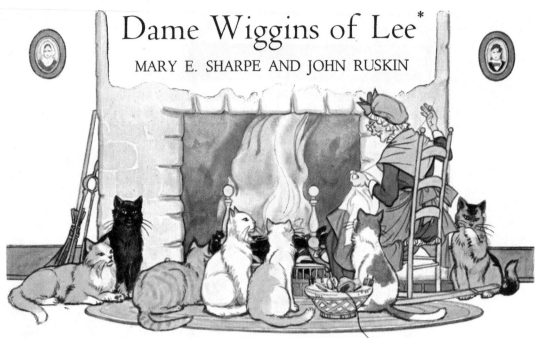

DAME Wiggins of Lee
 Was a worthy old soul,
As e'er threaded a nee-
 dle, or washed in a bowl;
She held mice and rats
 In such antipathee,
That seven fine cats
 Kept Dame Wiggins of Lee.

The rats and mice scared
 By this fierce whiskered crew,
The poor seven cats
 Soon had nothing to do;
So, as any one idle
 She ne'er loved to see,
She sent them to school,
 Did Dame Wiggins of Lee.

*The original verses of this famous old ballad are supposed to have been written by Mary E. Sharpe, an old lady of ninety and a friend of John Ruskin. Ruskin added many more verses and the ballad was first published, in 1823.

The master soon wrote
   That they all of them knew,
How to read the word "milk"
   And to spell the word "mew."
And they all washed their faces
   Before they took tea:
"Were there ever such dears!"
   Said Dame Wiggins of Lee.

When spring-time came back,
   They had breakfast of curds;
And were greatly afraid
   Of disturbing the birds.
"If you sit, like good cats,
   All seven in a tree,
They will teach you to sing!"
   Said Dame Wiggins of Lee.

So they sat in a tree,
  And said, "Beautiful! Hark!"
And they listened and looked
  In the clouds for the lark.
They sang, by the fireside,
  Symphoniouslee,
A song without words,
  To Dame Wiggins of Lee.

They called the next day
  On the tomtit and sparrow,
And wheeled a poor sick lamb
  Home in a barrow.
"You shall all have some sprats
  For your humanitee,
My seven good cats,"
  Said Dame Wiggins of Lee.

While she ran to the field
  To look for its dam,
They were warming its bed
  For the poor sick lamb.
They turned up the clothes
  All as neat as could be.
"I shall ne'er want a nurse,"
  Said Dame Wiggins of Lee.

She wished them good-night
  And went up to bed:
When, lo! in the morning,
  The cats were all fled.
The Dame's heart was nigh broke,
  So she sat down to weep,
When she saw them come back
  Each riding a sheep.

The Dame was unable
  Her pleasure to smother,
To see the sick lamb
  Jump up to its mother.
The farmer soon heard
  Where his sheep went astray,
And arrived at Dame's door,
  With his faithful dog Tray.

For the care of his lamb,
  And their comical pranks,
He gave them a ham
  And abundance of thanks.
"I wish you good-day,
  My fine fellows," said he;
"My compliments, pray,
  To Dame Wiggins of Lee!"

The Cock, the Mouse, and the Little Red Hen

FÉLICITÉ LE FÈVRE

ONCE upon a time there was a hill, and on the hill there was a pretty little house. It had one little green door, and four little windows with green shutters, and in it there lived *a cock* and *a mouse* and *a little red hen*. On another hill close by, there was another little house. It was very ugly. It had a door that wouldn't shut, and two broken windows, and all the paint was off the shutters. And in this house there lived *a bold bad fox* and *four bad little foxes*.

This story, slightly abridged, is used by permission of George W. Jacobs & Company.

THE LITTLE RED HEN

One morning these four bad little foxes came to the big bad Fox and said: "Oh, Father, we're so hungry!"

"We had nothing to eat yesterday," said one.

"And scarcely anything the day before," said another.

The big bad Fox shook his head, for he was thinking. At last he said in a big gruff voice: "On the hill over there, I see a house. And in that house there lives a Cock."

"And a Mouse!" screamed two of the little foxes.

"And a little Red Hen," screamed the other two.

"And they are nice and fat," went on the big bad Fox. "This very day, I'll take my sack and I will go up that hill and in at that door, and into my sack I will put the Cock and the Mouse and the little Red Hen."

So the four little foxes jumped for joy, and the big bad Fox went to get his sack ready to start upon his journey.

193

But what was happening to the Cock and the Mouse and the little Red Hen, all this time?

Well, sad to say, the Cock and the Mouse had both got out of bed on the wrong side that morning. The Cock said the day was too hot, and the Mouse grumbled because it was too cold.

They came grumbling down to the kitchen, where the good little Red Hen, looking as bright as a sunbeam, was bustling about.

"Who'll get some sticks to light the fire with?" she asked.

"I shan't," said the Cock.

"I shan't," said the Mouse.

"Then I'll do it myself," said the little Red Hen.

So off she ran to get the sticks.

"And now, who'll fill the kettle from the spring?" she asked.

"I shan't," said the Cock.

"I shan't," said the Mouse.

"Then I'll do it myself," said the little Red Hen.

And off she ran to fill the kettle.

194

"And who'll get the breakfast ready?" she asked, as she
put the kettle on to boil.

"I shan't," said the Cock.

"I shan't," said the Mouse.

"Then I'll do it myself,"
said the little Red Hen.

All breakfast time the Cock
and the Mouse quarrelled and
grumbled. The Cock upset

the milk jug, and the Mouse scattered crumbs upon the floor.

"Who'll clear away the breakfast?" asked the poor little
Red Hen, hoping they would soon leave off being cross.

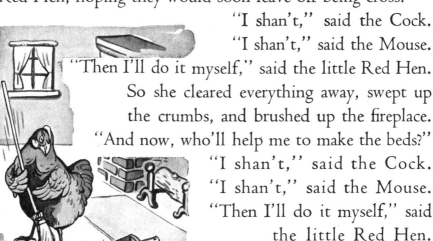

"I shan't," said the Cock.

"I shan't," said the Mouse.

"Then I'll do it myself," said the little Red Hen.
So she cleared everything away, swept up
the crumbs, and brushed up the fireplace.
"And now, who'll help me to make the beds?"

"I shan't," said the Cock.

"I shan't," said the Mouse.

"Then I'll do it myself," said
the little Red Hen.

And she tripped away upstairs.

But the lazy Cock and Mouse each sat down in a comfortable armchair by the fire, and soon fell fast asleep.

Now the bad Fox had crept up the hill and into the garden and, if the Cock and Mouse hadn't been asleep, they would have seen his sharp eyes peeping in at the window.

"Rat-tat-tat! Rat-tat-tat!" the Fox knocked at the door.

"Who can that be?" said the Mouse, half-opening his eyes.

"Look for yourself, if you must know," said the Cock.

"It's the postman, perhaps," thought the Mouse to himself, "and he may have a letter for me." So without waiting to see who it was, he lifted the latch and opened the door. As soon as he opened it, in jumped the big Fox. "Oh! Oh! Oh!" squeaked the Mouse, as he tried to run up the chimney.

"Doodle-doodle-doo!" screamed the Cock, as he jumped on the back of the biggest armchair.

196

But the Fox only laughed, and without more ado he took the little Mouse by the tail, and popped him into the sack, and seized the Cock by the neck and popped him in, too.

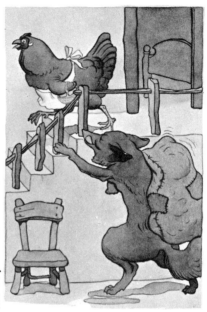

Then the poor little Red Hen came running downstairs to see what all the noise was about, and the Fox caught her and put her into the sack with the others. Then he took a long piece of string, wound it round and round and round the mouth of the sack, and tied it very tight indeed. After that he threw the sack over his back, and off he set down the hill, chuckling to himself.

"Oh, I wish I hadn't been so cross," said the Cock, as they went bumping about.

"Oh, I wish I hadn't been so lazy," said the Mouse, wiping his eyes with the tip of his tail.

"It's never too late to mend," said the little Red Hen. "And don't be too sad. See, I have my little workbag, and in it there is a pair of scissors and a little thimble and a needle and thread. Very soon you will see what I am going to do."

Now the sun was very hot, and soon Mr. Fox began to feel his sack was heavy, and at last he thought he would lie down under a tree and go to sleep for a little while. So he threw the sack down with a big bump and very soon fell fast asleep. Snore, snore, snore, went the Fox.

As soon as the little Red Hen heard this, she took out her scissors, and began to snip a hole in the sack just large enough for the Mouse to creep through.

"Quick!" she whispered to the Mouse. "Run as fast as you can and bring back a stone just as large as yourself."

Out scampered the Mouse, and soon came back, dragging the stone after him. "Push it in here!" said the little Red Hen, and he pushed it in, in a twinkling.

Then the little Red Hen snipped away at the hole, till it was large enough for the Cock to get through.

"Quick!" she said. "Run and get a stone as big as yourself."

Out flew the Cock, and soon came back quite out of breath, with a big stone, which he pushed into the sack, too. Then the little Red Hen popped out, got a stone as big as herself, and pushed it in. Next she put on her thimble, took out her needle and thread and sewed up the hole as quickly as ever she could.

THE LITTLE RED HEN

When it was done, the Cock and the Mouse and the little Red Hen ran home very fast, shut the door after and drew the bolts, shut the shutters, then drew down the blinds and felt quite safe.

The bad Fox lay fast asleep under the tree for some time, but at last he awoke.

"Dear, dear," he said, rubbing his eyes, "how late it is getting. I must hurry home."

So the bad Fox went grumbling and groaning down the hill, till he came to the stream. Splash! In went one foot. Splash! In went the other, but the stones in the sack were so heavy that at the very next step, down tumbled Mr. Fox into a deep pool. And then the fishes carried him off to their fairy caves and kept him a prisoner there, so he was never seen again. And the four greedy little foxes had to go to bed without any supper.

But the Cock and the Mouse never grumbled again. They lit the fire, filled the kettle, laid the breakfast, and did all the work, while the good little Red Hen sat resting in the big armchair. No foxes ever troubled them again; and, for all I know, they are still living happily in the little house with the green door and green shutters, which stands on the hill.

The Little Engine That Could

As told by Olive Beaupré Miller

ONCE there was a Train-of-Cars; she was flying across the country with a load of Christmas toys for the children who lived way over on the other side of the mountain. Her wheels went around very fast, squealing along on the track. Choo, choo! Choo, choo! Choo, choo! She was happy because she was carrying that load of toys for the children and she had just time enough to get to the end of her journey before the last Christmas shopping.

But, all of a sudden, bang! Right at the foot of the mountain the Little Engine broke down! Chug! Chug! Squeak! The wheels slid along the track and then stood perfectly still. She couldn't go an inch farther. And how in the world could she ever get across the mountains now in time for the children's Christmas?

LITTLE ENGINE THAT COULD

Rag dolls, paper dolls, china dolls, little toy wagons and carts, dolls' houses and Noah's arks, tops and bats and balls—were they all to stay there useless, and the children on the other side to go without them for Christmas? The little Train felt very sad as she stood there hoping for help. Then suddenly, toot, toot, toot! Along came a Great Strong Engine, all finely cleaned up and shining with his number plate scoured and bright. He had just finished his work of pulling a fine long passenger train, with sleeping cars and a dining-car. That was something to do! He was puffing and blowing with pride.

"O Big, Big Engine!" cried the Train while her Cars all joined in the chorus. "Will you please take us over the mountain? Our Engine has broken down, and we're loaded with Christmas toys for the children on the other side. Will you help us, help us, help us?"

But the Great Big Passenger Engine blew off steam with a shriek. He puffed himself up with pride. He made himself look very huge. "It's not my business," he roared, "to pull such a little nobody! I pull much finer trains with sleeping cars and a dining-car. I can't be bothered with you! Puff, puff! Ding, dong! Wheu-eu-eu!"

And he switched himself round on a sidetrack, passed the poor little Train-of-Cars and soon left her helpless, far behind. Well, the little Train-of-Cars felt sad but she never left off hoping that someone would come to help her.

Pretty soon, toot, toot! Along came a Great Strong Freight Engine. He had just pulled a freight train over the top of the mountain and was on his way back to the roundhouse to take a little rest. But the Train called to this Engine, too, while her Cars all joined in the chorus: "O Big, Big Engine, please, will you take us over the mountain? Our Engine has broken down, and we're loaded with Christmas toys for the children on the other side. Will you help us, help us, help us?"

But the Big Freight Engine snorted. He snorted and snorted and puffed. And he sent up out of his smokestack a shower of angry sparks. "I've done enough work for today! Yes-s-s S-s-sir-ee!" he hissed. "I'm off for a little res-s-st! I've done enough, done enough! I've done enough, done enough!"

And he switched himself round on the sidetrack, passed the poor little Train-of-Cars, and soon left her helpless far behind! Well, the little Train-of-Cars now felt very, very sad; but she never left off hoping that some one would come to help her.

Pretty soon dragging along there came slowly up the track a Rusty, Dusty, Dingy Engine, just about the size of

the Engine that had been pulling the Train. This Rusty, Dusty, Dingy Engine was sighing and moaning and grunting. He was rumbling and grumbling and groaning. But the little Train called out while her Cars all joined in the chorus: "O Engine, Engine, please, will you take us over the mountain? Our Engine has broken down and we're loaded with Christmas toys for the children on the other side. Will you help us, help us, help us?"

Then the Rusty, Dusty, Dingy Engine groaned and grunted and grumbled: "I never could pull you! I couldn't! I haven't the strength! No, No! I never could, I never could! I never could, I never could!" And he dragged himself round on the sidetrack, passed the poor little Train-of-Cars and soon left her helpless, far behind! Well, the little Train-of-Cars now felt very, very, very sad. Yet still she never stopped hoping that some one would come to help her.

LITTLE ENGINE THAT COULD

So after a long, long time, along came a Little Small Engine, an engine so very small it seemed useless to ask her for help; yet she had one bright, lively eye shining out in her head, and she was humming and hurrying, whistling and ringing her bell in the very liveliest way.

So the little Train cried out, while her Cars all joined in the chorus: "Little Engine, please, could you take us over the mountain? Our Engine has broken down, and we're loaded with Christmas toys for the children on the other side. Can you help us, help us, help us?"

Now the Little Small Engine had never been far away from the freight yard; she had spent all her days in switching. But think of all those children without their Christmas toys!

She couldn't let the Train stand still and the children have no toys for Christmas, so she started to chug up steam and she answered:

"*I think I can!*"

Then she came straight up to the Train, caught hold and started to pull! She tugged and she tugged and she pulled! And pretty soon, Ding, dong! Ding, dong! Puff, puff! Chug, chug! The Train-of-Cars began to move! Slowly, slowly, slowly the Train began to move! And the Little Small Engine kept toiling and tugging and tugging and pulling. And as she tugged she kept puffing, slowly, very slowly:

"I—think—I—can! I—think—I—can!"

Steadily she gained speed. And now she puffed out faster: "I-think-I-can! I-think-I-can! I-think-I-can!"

By and by she ran steadily, smoothly up the track and then she puffed very fast: "I think I can! I think I can! I think I can!"

206

At last, at last, and at last she reached the top of the mountain! She stood on top of the world! She'd climbed that big, long slope! She'd done it! She'd done it! She'd done it! And there, way down below, lay the city where the children lived to whom she was bearing the toys. She gave one puff of joy, just one great big long puff!

"*I thought I could!*" she puffed.

Then down she started sliding, faster, faster, faster. And as she went she kept puffing: "I thought I could! I thought I could! I thought I could! I thought I could! I thought I could! I thought I could!"

The little Train-of-Cars squealed merrily behind her and the children down in the city got their toys for Christmas.

Snow

LITTLE white feathers,
　Filling the air—
Little white feathers!
　How came you there?

"We came from the cloud-birds
　Sailing so high;
They're shaking their white wings
　Up in the sky."

Little white feathers,
　How swift you go!
Little white snowflakes,
　I love you so!

—Mary Mapes Dodge

Wee Robin's Christmas Song

FROM A SCOTCH FOLK TALE
ATTRIBUTED TO ROBERT BURNS

ONE bright, shiny Christmas morning, an old gray Pussy went out to walk to see what she could see. As she was walking along, pit-pat, through the snow, she saw a wee Robin Redbreast hopping about on a bush.

"Good morning, Robin," said she. "Where are you going on this cold and frosty morning?"

"I'm going to the King," answered the wee Robin Redbreast. "I'm going to sing him a song on this merry Christmas morning."

"Oh, but wait a minute before you go," said the old gray Pussy. "Just hop down here to me, and I'll show you a bonny white ring that I have around my neck."

But Robin looked down at Pussy with a twinkle in his eye. He knew she would like him for breakfast.

"Ha! ha! gray Pussy," said he, "you may show your white ring to the little gray mousie but I'll not wait a minute to let you show it to me! I'll go straight on to the King!"

So he spread his wings and flew away. He flew and he flew and he flew over the shiny white world till he came to a greedy old Hawk who was sitting on a fence.

"Good morning, Robin," cried the Hawk. "Where are you going on this cold and frosty morning?"

"I'm going to the King," answered the wee Robin Redbreast. "I'm going to sing him a song on this merry Christmas morning."

"Oh, but wait a minute before you go," said the greedy old Hawk. "I'll show you a bonny green feather I have here in my wing."

But the wee Robin saw the hungry look in the eye of the greedy old Hawk.

"Ha! ha! old Hawk," said he, "I saw you peck at the tiny birds, but I'll not wait a minute to let you peck at me. I'll go straight on to the King!"

So he spread his wings and flew away. And he flew and he flew and he flew until he came to a hillside where he saw a sly old Fox looking out of his hole.

"Good morning, Robin," said the Fox. "Where are you going on this cold and frosty morning?"

"I'm going to the King," answered the wee Robin Redbreast. "I'm going to sing him a song on this merry Christmas morning."

"Oh, but wait a minute before you go," said the sly old Fox. "Let me show you a queer black spot I have on the end of my tail."

"Ha! ha! sly Fox," said the Robin, "I saw you tease the wee lambie, and I'll not wait to see the queer black spot on your tail. I'll go straight on to the King."

So the Robin flew off once more and he flew and he flew and he flew until he saw a boy eating some bread and butter.

"Good morning, Robin," said the boy. "Where are you going on this cold and frosty morning?"

"I'm going to the King," answered the wee Robin Redbreast. "I'm going to sing him a song on this merry Christmas morning."

"Come a bit nearer," said the boy, "and I'll give you some crumbs from my bread."

"Nay, nay, my wee man," chirped the Robin. "I saw you catch the goldfinch, and I'll not wait for your crumbs. I'll go straight on to the King."

So, no matter who begged him to stop, the wee Robin paid no heed. He kept on about his business and flew straight off to the King. By and by he lit on the window sill of the palace. There he sat and he sang and so full of joy was he because this bright shiny morning was the blessed Christmasday, that he wanted the whole wide world to be as happy as he. He sang, and he sang, and he sang. The King and Queen sat at the window, and they were so pleased with his song that they asked each other what they could give to this sweet little singer, who had come so far to greet them.

"I know what we'll do," said the Queen. "We'll give him bonny wee Jenny Wren to be his mate."

So the King called for Jenny Wren, and Jenny Wren came flying. Then the wee, wee Robin and the wee, wee Wren sat side by side on the window sill, and they sang, and they sang, and they sang on that merry Christmas morning.

How Jenny Wren sings is beautifully depicted through the high, birdlike notes of the piccolo or octave flute in the short tone picture of the twittering little bird *The Wren* by Damare.

The Night Before Christmas*

CLEMENT MOORE

'TWAS the night before Christmas, when all
through the house
Not a creature was stirring, not even a mouse;
The stockings were hung by the chimney with care,
In hopes that St. Nicholas soon would be there;

The children were nestled all snug in their beds,
While visions of sugar-plums danced in their heads;
And Mamma in her kerchief, and I in my cap,
Had just settled our brains for a long winter's nap,

When out on the lawn there arose such a clatter,
I sprang from the bed to see what was the matter.
Away to the window I flew like a flash,
Tore open the shutters and threw up the sash.

*Written in 1823, by Dr. Clement Moore for his own family, this Christmas ballad is unique
in that it first introduced to American children the jolly old Santa Claus Dutch children knew.

The moon on the breast of the new-fallen snow
Gave the lustre of midday to objects below,
When, what to my wondering eyes should appear,
But a miniature sleigh, and eight tiny reindeer,

With a little old driver, so lively and quick,
I knew in a moment it must be St. Nick.
More rapid than eagles his coursers they came,
And he whistled, and shouted, and called them by name:

"Now, *Dasher!* now, *Dancer!* now, *Prancer* and *Vixen!*
On, *Comet!* on, *Cupid!* on, *Donner* and *Blitzen!*
To the top of the porch! to the top of the wall!
Now dash away! dash away! dash away all!"

As dry leaves that before the wild hurricane fly,
When they meet with an obstacle, mount to the sky,
So up to the house-top the coursers they flew,
With the sleigh full of Toys, and St. Nicholas, too.

And then, in a twinkling, I heard on the roof
The prancing and pawing of each little hoof.
As I drew in my head, and was turning around,
Down the chimney St. Nicholas came with a bound.

He was dressed all in fur, from his head to his foot,
And his clothes were all tarnished with ashes and soot;
A bundle of Toys he had flung on his back,
And he looked like a peddler just opening his pack.

His eyes how they twinkled! his dimples how merry!
His cheeks were like roses, his nose like a cherry!
His droll little mouth was drawn up like a bow,
And the beard of his chin was as white as the snow;

The stump of a pipe he held tight in his teeth,
And the smoke it encircled his head like a wreath;
He had a broad face and a little round belly,
That shook when he laughed, like a bowlful of jelly.

He was chubby and plump, a right jolly old elf,
And I laughed when I saw him, in spite of myself;
A wink of his eye and a twist of his head
Soon gave me to know I had nothing to dread.

He spoke not a word, but went straight to his work,
And filled all the stockings; then turned with a jerk,
And laying his finger aside of his nose,
And giving a nod, up the chimney he rose;

He sprang to his sleigh, to his team gave a whistle,
And away they all flew like the down of a thistle.
But I heard him exclaim, ere he drove out of sight,

Happy Christmas to All and to All a Good Night!

Merry Christmas

AT Christmas play and make good cheer,
For Christmas comes but once a year.

—*The Farmers' Daily Diet by Thomas Tusser, 16th Century*

HEAP on more wood,
The wind is chill;
But let it whistle as it will,
We'll keep our Christmas merry still!

—*Sir Walter Scott*

I HEARD the bells on Christmas Day
Their old, familiar carols play,
And wild and sweet
The words repeat
Of peace on earth, good-will to men!

—*Henry Wadsworth Longfellow*

For many centuries, English children have celebrated Christmas by decorating houses with holly and mistletoe, bringing the yule log in from the forest, and singing carols like *God Rest Ye Merry Gentlemen.*

The Tale of Nutcracker[*]

BASIS OF THE BALLET BY PETER TCHAIKOVSKY

ON Christmas Marie and her brothers had a fine big Christmas tree. It shone with lighted candles. Its branches were draped with strings of popcorn and hung with honey-cakes, sugar-plums, oranges, cookies, candy, dolls, tin soldiers and many other toys. The children's mother and father, with a crowd of merry guests, all gathered around the tree to give the presents out. But, while they were doing this, jolly Uncle Thomas came in quite loaded down with gifts. To each of the children he gave a doll that could walk and talk; but to Marie, he handed another wonderful gift, the one she liked best of all. It was a wooden nutcracker having the head of a man who cracked nuts between his jaws.

How Marie loved that nutcracker! She carried it around in her arms till her little brother, Fritz, snatched it from her and broke it. Marie burst into tears. She picked up the broken nutcracker, and soothed him in her arms. Then she put him in a little doll's cradle and gently rocked him to sleep.

[*]Tchaikovsky wrote the music of his *Nutcracker Suite* as a ballet for Russian children to dance. "The Dance Characteristique" is a toy march around the Christmas tree and suggests dolls and tin soldiers.

THE TALE OF NUTCRACKER

When the Christmas party was over, the candles were all put out and the family went up to bed. But Marie could not go to sleep for thinking of her nutcracker. At last she got up quietly and stole down the stairs to see him. But what did she see now? The Christmas tree grew up tall before her eyes. Again it was all a great blaze of light. The dolls and the other toys came down from the branches where they hung and started in to dance. And Marie heard music, gay lively music, with the piping of shrill little flutes and the silver chiming of bells.

M S HURFORD

The toys were all dancing merrily to that music when suddenly there came scampering into the room an army of little mice. They had come to eat up the sweets that still hung on the tree. So the toys lined up in a hurry. Led by Nutcracker, they started to fight the army of mice. What a battle they fought! It was a terrific tussle. At last, King Mouse, the leader of the band of tiny robbers, fought hand to hand with Nutcracker. Then little Marie, afraid that her beloved Nutcracker might get hurt in the fray, threw her shoe at King Mouse. Instantly the mice scattered, running in all directions and scampering off to their holes.

But now that the battle was over, a very strange thing happened. Nutcracker all at once changed into a man, a fine young prince. Politely he bowed and kissed the hand of little Marie, and he asked her to fly with him far away to a beautiful place full of goodies, a place that was called Jam Mountain. Jam Mountain! Oh, Jam Mountain! What little girl would not like to fly to such a place? Marie said yes at once and off they went on their way.

THE TALE OF NUTCRACKER

They flew over forests and plains in company with the fluffy little white fairy snowflakes and soon they reached Jam Mountain.

What a land that was! It had a mountain of strawberry jam with piles of sugar on top. All kinds of candy came running to meet them and along with the candy, a lovely little lady, the Sugar-Plum Fairy, came flying on shining wings. Gaily she greeted the Prince and Marie. Then a great feast was held in their honor. The green and yellow stick candies and the pink-and-white striped stick candies and the chocolates, and other goodies all began to dance. Even brown coffee-berries from Java, and dignified tea leaves from China, joined in the merrymaking.

M·S·HURFORD·

Flowers danced a gay little waltz.* The toy pipes danced a
polka and the Sugar-Plum Fairy herself went lightly tripping
and twirling, skipping and twinkling and sparkling, nodding
her head and bowing most prettily to Marie. Again there
was sprightly music, lively, brisk, and gay.

But, just at that moment, Marie suddenly opened her eyes.
In the moonlight she saw the snow lying white on neighboring rooftops, the bare black branches of trees, laden down
with the snow and little soft drifts of snowflakes piled high
on her window sill. Where was she? What a surprise! She was
not in the land of the gay little Sugar-Plum Fairy. She was

lying on her own little bed upstairs
in her own little room and she
had only been dreaming! And
Nutcracker? What of Nutcracker?
He was in his cradle where she
would find him in the morning.

*The *Waltz of the Flowers* has lovely harp music and the *Dance of the Sugar-Plum Fairy* is full of
sparkling gaiety. In the *Dance of the Toy Flutes*, the piccolo or little flute can be heard.

The Sugar-Plum Tree*

EUGENE FIELD

HAVE you ever heard of the Sugar-Plum Tree?
'Tis a marvel of great renown:
It blooms on the shore of the Lollypop sea
In the garden of Shut-Eye Town;
The fruit that it bears is so wondrously sweet
(As those that have tasted it say)
That good little children have only to eat
Of that fruit to be happy next day.

When you've got to the tree you would have a hard time
To capture the fruit which I sing;
The tree is so tall that no person could climb
To the boughs where the sugar-plums swing:
But in that tree sits a chocolate cat,
And a gingerbread dog prowls below—
And this is the way you contrive to get at
Those sugar-plums tempting you so.

You say but the word to that gingerbread dog,
And he barks with such terrible zest
That the chocolate cat is at once all agog,
As her swelling proportions attest.
And the chocolate cat goes cavorting around
From this leafy limb unto that,
And the sugar-plums tumble, of course, to the ground—
Hurrah for that chocolate cat!

There are marshmallows, gumdrops, and peppermint canes
With stripings of scarlet or gold,
And you carry away of the treasure that rains,
As much as your apron can hold:
So come, little child, cuddle closer to me
In your dainty white nightcap and gown,
And I'll rock you away to that Sugar-Plum Tree,
In the garden of Shut-Eye Town.

J
808.8   My storytime treasure
M

DEMCO